Texas

Texas

Claudio Gaudio

QUATTRO BOOKS

The publication of *Texas* has been generously supported by the Canada Council for the Arts and the Ontario Arts Council.

Canada Council for the Arts Conseil des Arts du Canada

ONTARIO ARTS COUNCIL
CONSEIL DES ARTS DE L'ONTARIO

Cover design: Andre Jodoin
Editor: John Calabro
Typography: Grey Wolf Typography

Library and Archives Canada Cataloguing in Publication

Gaudio, Claudio
Texas / Claudio Gaudio.

Issued also in an electronic format.

ISBN 978-1-927443-09-5

I. Title.

PS8613.A918T49 2012 C813'.6 C2012-903898-9

Published by Quattro Books Inc.
382 College Street
Toronto, Ontario, M5T 1S8
www.quattrobooks.ca

Printed in Canada

For Carlos, my Son
and fellow saboteur

1

My exit was no laughing matter, torn as I was from the shores of a superpower. When I was called to the Capital I knew I was headed for much smaller quarters than my Manhattan office, but I could never have imagined this stall, a room smack-dab in the middle of a massacre. Before I left, the butcher showed me how to make the best cut. I bought vitamins and a gun, said goodbye to my mother, consulted with my doctor, cheated on my wife and shot a small animal. I put it all in my report and prepared to meet the President. He informed me that my death would be trivial but necessary. My accountant assured me he would invest the proceeds. I changed all the dates, dug up my father's bones and hid them in the attic. I was free.

When I got here George's thunder rolled, the rich were leaving for France and the dead could speak. My advisor was a man at the disposal of the coalition except when he was transporting Afghan heroin up his ass. He told me that his eyes block the future and it is difficult to find a good firing squad in the middle of a morning milking. I didn't understand a word he said and later I realized it just didn't matter. Happily my bewilderment did not preclude us from becoming friends. His name was Aban. This country is my orchard, he said, if you put it in a box it will shrink every distance and Texas cannot adapt to small spaces. Sorry for the invasion, I said, the good news is we have no plan for the occupation. Our best estimate is just a few weeks. We do what we do, and then we discover the reason. It's a blind man's technique. We'll leave after the contracts are signed.

It was in New York that I accepted my mission. Two Texas couriers walked past the café, a fruit stand, a tobacconist, and dog people scattered to both sides of the boulevard. Up four floors of a brownstone to my office overlooking a courtyard with old trees where squirrels lived and birds came to visit. They were an odd pair, one small, a touch overweight and impeccably groomed, the other tall, slim and dishevelled. The tall man placed a briefcase on my desk, I already had the combination. The document began and ended with please advise as to your earliest departure. I placed a note in the case and scrambled the tumblers. The smaller man picked it up, we'll see you there, he said … where, I said … that's classified.

In the morning there was a car at my door. The driver handed me a plane ticket to the Nation's Capital, executive class. There will be another car when you land, he said. The Capital was all fancy chocolates, the rustle of girls' skirts through a wheat field. One of them showed me a dictionary and pointed to the words that were missing. Only these are good for planting, she said. I wanted to disagree but she took my head in her hands which were clean as ivory. These are the hours we will teach you to forget, she said, now sleep while I read to you from the book of last things. This is what evenings are like in the Capital, tea and biscuits, the end elsewhere, a rumour from a faraway puddle.

I am a diplomat, a messenger in the mouth of what is already here, of what has already been said. Each morning I cut a deal with my reflection and then I watch as he picks up the razor. When I'm not travelling I live in New York. New York is in Texas. I speak many languages, perhaps all of them, and have access to vast lists and addresses. In Galilee I turned a carpenter into a king. I was there when the British and the French raided your village. In El Salvador I turned death squads into freedom fighters and farmers into rebels. In Iran I armed the government and the government in waiting. During negotiations I keep the car running with plenty of cash in the trunk. The Air Force will clarify what I can't explain.

When I arrived at the Capital the President was in the library and a film crew was rolling up cables and carefully placing equipment into hard metal cases. They were preparing to leave. The Commander-in-Chief looked a little lost and felt compelled to explain the venue was the choice of his handlers. Hell, he said, everyone knows I'm not a scholar ... yes sir, Mr. President. He was happy I'd come and told me I'd be going away to the war. I was to scrub the names and change the numbers, or the other way around, before they were sent back to Texas. Mr. President, I can do that from New York … we must find our reasons there and rattle them here … what are our reasons … whatever you say they are … yes of course.

The next morning I took a helicopter to a military plane. Its cargo was soldiers inside the packs on their backs. I was in my briefcase. The soldiers had already been told what to do, I told them what not to say after they did it. On landing I met our partners from England and a few from Australia. The Swedes were not represented. A sergeant from Wyoming escorted me to a convoy of armoured vehicles waiting at the edge of the airstrip, engines running. On leaving I noticed the soldiers unpacking and repacking their gear, repeatedly to master a gesture that might soon be their last. Eventually the trucks came to take them to their final destination. The sergeant informed me that he had been charged with my safety. We have a situation, he said. He needed someone who spoke the resident language and would I be kind enough to lend my assistance … yes of course.

We drove a short distance to a two-room house on the periphery of a small cluster of similar dwellings. A well stood ten or so metres from the back door. An old man was sitting on the porch under a sheet-metal awning. What does he want to tell us, asked the sergeant. The man explained there was a dead soldier inside the well. How did he get there … he was shooting at everyone … that's not good … that's what I told him … how did he get inside the well … I shot him … that's a problem … I know … how old are you … eighty-seven … why did you shoot the soldier … he killed my son. What did he say, asked the sergeant … he said one of your soldiers is dead inside the well … we know that, how did he get there … he doesn't know … did he see anything … no … tell him someone will come to collect the body. The sergeant thanked him, hearts and minds, he said, with a grin. I told the old man never to repeat his story.

We left the old man standing in the doorway. Through the small windows of the armoured car I could see the city, shattered glass and fallen masonry. I was driven to a secure complex comprised of several square miles. It was the palace of the previous king and now a little piece of Texas organized in the spirit of a college campus – dormitories, bars and fast food chains. Post-adolescents on the up side of a high school touchdown and before their first blowjob are sent here to flicker and die. When they went to collect the soldier inside the well the old man was dead. A bullet through the right side of his skull to match the report. That's how we knew it was suicide. Now he's small talk, scuttlebutt working its way through the cafeteria. Eventually he'll be a story in Wyoming.

I was assigned an office with a bedroom adjacent. There were televisions in both rooms to make sure we were all watching the same war. The floor and the walls were marble, the ceilings plaster. The echo was distracting and distorted the music that I had so carefully selected to get me through all of this. The soldier responsible for my comfort managed to find me a very fine stereo. I asked him for some carpeting to absorb the sound, anything will do, I said. The next day he delivered four large, fine Persian rugs. I only need two … I can't take them back … I see, put one on the floor and hang one on the wall of each room … which walls … opposite the door … which rugs … you look like you have a flair for this … yes sir.

Bartok packed a lunch and a gramophone and set himself to wandering. He went digging for the old songs, the old stories. They were floating face down in the Danube a few steps ahead of the secret police. Now he holds the darker chords a little longer. He is his father, he is his father's father and the toothless grin of the Huns. In Budapest they say he didn't just lick it off the ground. I have yet to hear God speak – a little vibration in the larynx, thoughts lost to thoughts otherwise. On earth music trumps conversation. In the war to end all wars one thing led to another and then the corpses began to pile up. It is best to catalogue bodies before they are buried. Listen, if you will, to the music a man with a shovel makes.

Before leaving the Capital I was called to the office of the press secretary. His name was Scott, but the President, who was fond of nicknames, called him Fuckface. There was a television in his office too. On screen a journalist was interviewing another rugged and dusty general on the difficulties of a winning strategy. Scott pointed to the screen, that's the war that matters, he said, the one we're fighting. The war on the ground will take care of itself. He was short on detail and admitted that sometimes things change, a little. He made no apology for machines that rust in the desert, for compounds that poison the sea. He made no apology for the winning team.

The President is finding it hard to respect a man he calls Fuckface. The press secretary's job is to deliver public opinion with an accomplished lack of interest. In his back pocket are several enormous and widespread academics. They won't talk to each other but a brain cell will consult with its neighbour for a second opinion. What do you think ... that depends, what do you think. The enemy, I heard Scott say, will be severely wanting in democracy and sanctions for oil. A healthy child death rate will be maintained by the purposeful contamination of water, without favouritism. Vaccines are weapons-grade biological agents and will not be distributed. Tried and proper instruments of state we will later deny.

2

The day I left, the President spoke plainly. Make history, he said, but first meet your quotas. The problem, it seems, was in my translation. My initial orders were to cancel local elections, make a list of those who would testify against the language, look for anthrax in the kitchen, submarines in the desert and missiles inside paper lanterns. At least that's what I heard. Upon submitting my report, I was further instructed to record the coordinates of factories still standing and their capacity to get in the way of the money, or what the contractors here called the real money. I was given discretion to meet with spokespeople of every description, and relay promises and threats. Clean the streets and distribute food for the camera, nothing in the thousands, things among things.

The day after my arrival Aban reported for work. When he was not with me or scouring the hills of Afghanistan he sold Western trinkets in a bombed-out building fifty or so yards from the palace. A distance now measured in the blessed calculus of a smart bomb. I live by the knife, he said, for fear of losing his Texan stipend. His job was to help distribute shrink-wrapped cash from Texas to the people he knew could influence events. The money arrived with Swiss precision, armoured and burlapped for favour and sway. Aban dispensed it, at his whim and pleasure, from a plastic chair in the courtyard of our office next to the market. He decided what their stories were worth, I collected the words and sent them back to Texas.

Every morning Aban insisted that we leave before lunch. For breakfast we would have tea, and biscuits he pulled from his pocket, two for me, and two for him. He refused to eat in the cafeteria. There is pork and the food is shit. Our meals were prepared daily by his friends who worked in the market. As we ate he gave voice to every thought in his head, his tongue rummaging the ashes for information a diplomat might not uncover. The secret, he said, is what we want and cannot have, is what we are. Apparently we don't have an eye for beginnings, and what follows understanding is death. At day's end he gave me my dinner, wrapped, to eat in my room.

Today is Sunday, or Monday, between sunup and sunset is where I look for the things that I could stop doing. I'm saving the nights for when there are none. I came to this country with notion and syntax to bridge a massacre, to reconcile events with their non-occurrence. I do not know that now, now I am only here. In a car it seems, there was some shooting. My capture was a simple unfolding, certain and without ceremony. I was hooded and tied in the first rays of an autumn sun. Aban died without a whisper while sitting on a plastic chair in the sights of an adolescent in Nike shoes and the bandana to match, brandishing an AK-47. A reliable gun and my favourite because the inventor also wrote poetry. In Aban's hand was the blade that he lived by.

If you're looking for justification, Carl Rove once told me, it is best to work backwards from what is intended. Our reasons for invading this country were formed of empty imaginings and perfectly timed for the next election. It takes a war to prevent a war. In anguish a man will cut his neighbour but he won't face a tank with a slingshot. A child will. Children are stronger than tanks. My job was to show these people that they could not escape our stake in this place. Honour and valour, right foot march, right foot, right foot, this will be the best campaign ever. I have served, among other places, in Compton and Detroit. I watched and reported what the people were saying as they set fire to themselves.

In Westminster Abbey it is said that God and Empire do not rejoice in the annihilation of the living. The day before they killed Lorca I told him he would live forever. Truth makes a mockery of death. On my way to London or Istanbul I decided all explanation is an affront to affliction. I used to carry a map of the last several centuries charted by hunchbacks, poets who would empty a glass and move slowly through the fire. I have been speaking with those who lived before me on the streets of British Calcutta. They have risen and are living within striking distance of Notting Hill. What of our legacy they ask. Your affairs have been cancelled, your children have received the new king.

This is an ancient city, my abductors are calm and focused on the route vanishing in the cuts, the flaws of dead engineers. I'm looking to slip through the zero in their calculations. Knotted and blindfolded I cannot brace or anticipate the car's turning. I am a rag in a Mercedes with a reputation for holding the road. But for the soldiers on either side I would fly into the wind, a brief stopover in Paris perhaps and then on to New York. In the courtyard Aban's friends will have closed his eyes, covered him in clean white linen. If not for our collaboration he'd be on his way to paradise, but I don't think he'd be happy there. It's too simple a place.

For these good soldiers, my captors, there are situations until the end. They have no need for the coming century because there was one before this one, and better dynasties. Jewelled virgins and pillows, silk birds under heaven will show them the way home, and the line they cannot cross. In the car we evade near encounters with Texas patrols and review protocol. The prospect of being pulled over provokes only fear, as I would be killed immediately, a toll to the hereafter. The instructions are as follows: if captured, the combatant to my right will kill me, if he is killed first the responsibility will shift to the left. The last man standing will kill the wounded, if any, and then himself – got it.

On arrival everyone is a little unhinged but pleased to be reunited with others who I assume are part of the same fighting unit. They are stationed in what seems to be a large stately residence transplanted from Boston or the English countryside. I cannot account for its wood structure or red brick facade. Clearly it had known better days. On the roof is a tarp, the aluminium eaves and steel railings have been picked clean and probably sold for scrap. A youngish man in his early thirties brings food and water, collects ancillary weapons and gear from two cars that had been equipped for my capture.

They call him Hakim. He sets up a tripod and a camera in a small supplementary building while the celebration of my abduction subsides. In time there will be demands and no discussion, silence open and abundant.

After the filming Hakim escorted me to my prison room. A kitchen, large and clear for the pacing that will gather the day and scatter the night. An appendage to the main house, an afterthought with no consideration given to a Victorian aesthetic. The door is a wood slab secured by rusting hardware, the walls grey stone and mortar. In the middle hangs a naked bulb. Against the wall opposite the door is a stone fireplace with logs half eaten, hooks for small game and a table with two chairs that don't match, torn. Ancient pots blackened and pending from a steel grid, blacker still over wine-spattered concrete. In a corner lies a simple cot. There are cracks from the war and a small window to see the east rising. I begin in the west. The stones under my feet are irregular but I measure the posting of each step to forget it.

When I am not pacing I sit in silence, in the condition of such and such a person missing, one among millions. The future is rusting beneath the thistle, gaining on some abandoned railroad. When I came to this country I was armed to the teeth, that's how they knew I was friendly. They will kill me. I am an envoy of trifling status and of no consequence to either side of the question. They have a camera, a script, a corpse and then another – basic things. On arrival I am cast and made to kneel. The story will be tendered first to Texas, an exchange that will not be made and then to some gaping deity. It is important my performance be sincere, quietly I rehearse the script. I do not want to die. Cut to this room where I will wait, but I don't mind the delay. There are so many things on which I can meditate.

3

On the other side of these walls doctors are analyzing flying lungs and limbs, they are hoping not to lose an entire generation. Texas, before you got here these people parked cars and kept a record of every disaster. In the desert calligraphy flattens to a deep purple memory, nightmares and images in the belly and the brains. Poems, prayers and knives stockpiled in the school yard. They are attending meetings in municipal gardens next to open sewers, there never seem to be enough buildings. There is no air, just broken promises and a dizzying display of coffins. Texas, all is gain. All the signs have been lost to yesterday's news, the horizon disbanded, the years dispersed in a bed of bones. Everything is ready for you to fix it.

In the morning Hakim brought soap and a basin filled to the brim with clean water. A few hours later he brought coffee, two books and a bowl of raisin bran. A guard stood at the door. I was the next story in the room. There will be one meal a day, said Hakim, and it will come in the afternoon. I will bring enough food so there's a little left over for the evening, nuts usually and a few pieces of fruit for the morning … thank you but I'm not here to discuss food … oh … I demand to know my proximity to the nullity that is now occurring … I see … there must be some mistake … I don't think so … perhaps you've not seen my wingspan … your what … I'm friends with the President and his press secretary, Fuckface … I see … have you ever heard a Texas dog howl … a few. Hakim didn't seem to hear my questions and so I was forced to consider the possibility I hadn't asked them, but that doesn't explain why he refused me the information.

I watched him cover the bed with a light blanket. He put the soap and basin next to the fireplace, a plate, cup and some books on the counter. I had the impression that all of these things had been here before. Why the books, I asked … they are from previous prisoners … I see … I am learning to speak

English … oh … perhaps you will help me … yes of course … I am Hakim … I know who you are, who is the man at the door … he doesn't want you to know his name … this is an odd house … it was built by an Englishman in 1917 … I see … it was to be his country residence … oh … but he never lived in it … why … he died suddenly of cholera … I see … tomorrow we will begin our lessons … yes of course … I will bring you soup … thank you.

The people were calm as the bombs fell in the courtyard. Aban quietly put away the money. He knew the city no longer had the tools to break through the steel and concrete slabs. Knocking and voices were heard for days. Each time there is only this time, he said, and our day will come. As for myself, I had hoped to be in a bar sipping whisky, having run out of prospects, putting on a little glow to make sense of the din. Moderation is a difficult thing, and not much will come of it. At the moment of our end there is nothing. It is a well fed, well fucked Texas pilot, ready to do the town. Nothing but blue skies next to the almighty, and steel. As for events on the ground, we'll just have to invent them.

It's easy to lose oneself during an air raid, stealth jets restless and breathing, more idea than object against the setting sun. A roar from inside the clouds and all directions approaches without colour, without form. Houses briefly gather in their windows, a flood of perfect light empties beneath blind cement. Who is seeing this? Celestial campaigns reinvent time and distance, irretrievable like a face forgotten inside a mirror, the music of Beethoven all at once. The clash of civilizations will go on and the good book will focus our attention, keep the formation of the stars and the heavens. If God were here he'd pull these planes down from the sky, but the bastard doesn't exist.

Aban is dead now, it was me they wanted. He was motionless while his killer approached. He liked drama, his own luck on the head of a pin. He was a fan of Hollywood in the forties – Bogart, because he didn't talk much. He hated the fifties. Nothing but the years ahead and a garage full of small appliances waiting for the weekend. Things aren't built to last anymore, they're not worth fixing. Dad can go straight to drinking. Christmas trees matched the tinsel, made by Dow Chemical and like so many things it came in a spray. It's the decade that gave us aluminium siding, thanks to the war. Soon everything would last forever, we thought, including mom's breasts. In 1961 Dow's little brother Corning invented the silicone implant.

You must go away, said Aban ... why ... because you're killing all the people. I have lost what was said and what was done. People are hiding in the millions, behind borders, the wreckage of demarcation. The plural is how we hollow out a population, it's just easier to kill by the thousands. Some will eat, some will starve and some will have never been here. I put it all in my report. Aban disagrees with the numbers but the President thinks they're fine. We return the flesh to its elements, circumvent the funeral, and the burial is instantaneous. The fear is real, the pain of others will pass, try to muddle on. We each must cope as best we can, as we eat, sleep and are annihilated.

In this room I live inside the shoebox I keep underneath my bed, or is it in my head? It doesn't matter, I just need some place to put things so that I can take them out again. This is where I keep the first snowfall and the promise I made to myself, to die in Paris. This only, and the hope, the scent of a visit, preferably from the waitress at the all-night diner rather than a higher power. Each time I talk to God he just doesn't get it. Birth is an expulsion into a place that is missing, a fabric without weave or measure. It's the laughter that sticks in your throat. I am an immigrant. I lied about meeting the President. Wait, I am not done. Here are the words that will save you: *he* will die and you are not him.

I once knew a poet from Saskatchewan, in Saskatchewan this is how every story begins. On his deathbed he told me he'd had a good life. There, in the colonies, a bard can still get a drink for a pun but the metaphors have been thoroughly picked over. Happily they still have an ear for a rhyme. The truth, he once told me, is in the long dead winters where we live. Life is a sickness, he said, I will go to India, or was it Peru. There, on the edge of impossible cities I will be nobody's son. The truth will fly out of my mouth as I listen to the sound of the ancients dreaming, backwards. Then he explained that the next best English novelist will be from Mumbai. His grammar will be impeccable, he said, but in Exeter they know he will be more diligent than able.

After the Second World War we needed to contain Chinese expansion. Social change is contagious and sufficient to establish intent, countries were falling like dominos. We needed to protect the people of Indochina from the governments they were electing. In Vietnam we learned that it is difficult to dislodge an administration from its constituency, so long as the constituency continues to exist. What is good for Texas is good for the world. In Russia they're thinking of Stalin again since Gorbachev tore down the wall. Eastern Europe is the new Trojan horse from which Texas will dismantle the region. Free at last, free at last, who needs the Mexicans now that we have the Ukrainians.

These days ritual murder will not secure the harvest, it will do nothing to rouse the Queen's uterus, it has never kept our enemies at bay. The two criteria of a legitimate target are that it be defenseless and that they have something we want. After we defeated Hitler we kicked the French out of the Middle East and sent them to Africa. In 1951 Japan was made to pay reparations for their war of aggression against China. The cheque was made payable to Texas. Fifty years later, the same treaty was used to protect American subsidiaries against lawsuits from Asian victims of Japanese fascism. Texas' favourite countries are a little bigger than a breadbox. International law is there to be broken, errant numbers and random skin. We will teach you to torture your own.

I knew where to look from my Manhattan condo, I rallied the young while I dined on truffles and wine. War is a beautiful idea. I am the one who put the Huns in the saddle, showed them how to make two cups from one skull. Next to the dead, eyes and lips moisten, in this room I walk on the tip of my tongue. Yesterday a bird told me I could continue my dictation so long as it doesn't make sense. That's fine, since I will not be the one reading it and writing it slows the next thing from happening. Everything and anything comes out of my mouth, so I wouldn't call this a voice. What I know of the world is smaller than the gap between two words, but I'm learning to spit.

Lord knows this will not be a long life, but there have been such moments. It does not matter the name, that he is, or is not. That he is eternal. God is not what we see but all we penetrate, that's why he's so hard to get rid of. I used to think dicing onions and washing dishes was a waste of time, now I peel every grape. My first and last thoughts are elsewhere, and so are the ones in between. People are alright when they live and work according to their nature, searching and not finding. There is enough time amid the bombs falling. The window in this room has three bars that cut the sky, portals to a courtyard where two chickens and a goat wait to be killed. They feed without lifting their heads.

I am not now, nor have I ever been, a chicken or a goat. I am neither for nor against their destruction, yet they are changed forever by my gaze and by this sentence. It is the name that makes chickens and goats possible, pins them to their absence, of which death, and I hesitate to state the obvious, is but a small part. I stood at the window and watched them but I wish to remain flexible on the time and the date. That's how I know I'm living in the hereafter. The twentieth century is now on the shelf. One hundred years can't fill a thimble and no message was left. For a while we walked lightly in blue jeans and sandals, in what looked like another beginning. As for God, he knew he was dead before he read Nietzsche. He was just trying to stay current.

4

THINKING CANNOT HOLD ME. Ready, steady – go. Lewis Paul Bremer III once ran the Boston Marathon in three hours and thirty-four seconds. He had a plaque on his desk which read success has a thousand fathers, failure is an orphan. He never got over the regret of those last thirty-four seconds. The only thing that seemed to help was bombing Baghdad. He doesn't run anymore but he walks with the dexterity of a seasoned footman. He serves the President, who, in turn, looks to Bremer for what there is to think. For his birthday the Commander-in-Chief gave Bremer a sandbox, and then he filled it with children. They will come to be known as the next generation of those who died young long ago. Bremer is happy in his new great big life. Everyone calls him the viceroy and he likes to watch the troops marching. He will address the President's concerns after his cucumber salad.

For the reconstruction the viceroy wore gloves and a hardhat. Aban and I always arrived before him and told everyone else what he needed to hear. Off the record, the city was burning. Then we were driven back to the green zone, past several guards, a metal detector and a few tanks. We were members of the strategic communications team. We decided what occasions had sufficient gravity to warrant leaving the palace. The backdrop to the podium from which we advised Texas was draped in blue canvas and peppered with stars. A line of flags behind the speaker, and on the podium itself, the eagle. It was designed by the President's own image consultant. One day the viceroy decided to burn this country's notes and print new money to pay for the war. The new dinar has security features to discourage counterfeiting and can be purchased at National City Bank, 2007 South MacArthur Boulevard, Springfield, Illinois.

Here is a short list of things that I know: an exergue is the base or basis on the reverse side of a coin where the emblem or the signature is struck. The obverse is the face. Parricide is the murder of a close relative. Musing is the work of separation. That's it, but there will be more lists later. A lot of thought has gone into money. Before Eve reached for the apple she was in Atlantic City. She examined coins. She foresaw smartly dressed orgasms over the phone and a black dog on a leash. I will be the wind in a burning building, she thought. Her dreams fit inside this paragraph. If you turn the page she will run from the window that faces the sun. Suddenly, satiated, she is afraid.

There are a lot of numbers in the previous few paragraphs and this one. If I ever get out of here we will all go to the museum and stand next to history. Then you will know what I know. From behind the glass I will show you again what we cannot bear. Outside my window there are three palm trees whistling beyond the courtyard, beyond the corner's turn. I walk to and from the window. I am what I cannot see. The invisible rises to greet me, right foot forward, I do not move. It is best if we do not go back to the war, it is broken and I cannot hold it in time. I'm trying to work but from this room I can't get anything done, neither life nor art. War will not be reduced.

On the morning before my capture two men entered my office with a woman who lives in this city. They held her arms to stop her from tearing at her face and hair. Her children had not come home from school, it was bombed during math class. I gave her money, she did not understand. I am a prisoner now, no one else and me together at last and soon to be seen talking to a dead bird. In the beginning was the word and the rest I don't understand. As for the kids, it was an accident. They are with me now, or so I imagine, fluttering about baskets of ripened figs that I hold playfully above their reach. With a grab and a shriek they fly like bandits, like angels to lie on the cool concrete. They enact scenes of battle against armies who would scatter their ashes to a world much larger than a house and a garden.

Is a week longer than a day?

A mountain yawns, fells a city and wraps itself in a grapevine. There are exits death does not know. Every night Hakim locks the door and quickly, before I am afraid, I'm through the courtyard, into the street and on my way to Pompeii. I have decided to rescue that city's entire population. On arrival slaves bring me flowers and I assure them that exile does not end with death, it continues. This is called an enigma. From Pompeii I fly to Paris where I settle for a shower and a better hotel room, smaller than the room I'm in, but in Paris they change the sheets. Then it's back to the war. In Hollywood it is spread with the same bloody trowel, in Flint, Michigan it's a story told from the inside of a coffin. In my room I know now how each day begins. One guest brings another, and food is issued in adequate amounts.

Hakim tells me my last words will be recorded, and transmitted all over the world ... will they be heard in New York, I ask ... yes of course. But first they will be clipped and squeezed through my teeth and distilled again to fit through a wire racing beneath some ocean and then pole to pole. There's no need to write it all down as though it were a message that could be understood later. It's a refusal. I wanted to die later and preferably not on cable. Deaf and balding perhaps, in some more or less insignificant building. By then I would have updated the casualty list and the number of people living in tents. I would have listed every rape, every lynching and everyone who disappeared under a bus, closed the gap between numbers and bones.

I remember the snow in New York receding during a late winter rain. The ground scarred and hesitant, pulling itself in to the fore. It is cool in my room and at night it retains the heat. They build for the climate here. A rodent scuttles by my feet, glimpses my end, and at least for now it is reluctant to speak. A jostled creature in a constant state of astonishment. In Manhattan we imagined them as under the wheels of a subcompact. There, where each night I emptied my plate and then the bottle, only to awaken my greed for a woman's knee. I will not be forgiven for what she helped me forget. Last night there were two of us, please come find me again.

After I sleep, perhaps, Hakim enters and engages what I assume are my ideas. Evers and nevers in between naps. He's talking to me, that much is certain. Behind my eyes my brain is constantly working. That's how I know who is speaking. The guards no longer accompany his visits but from other rooms their voices still pierce the silence. When I hear them walking I freeze, breathe, only after I fix their direction. Hakim is asking if there are messages, he will see to it that they reach their destination. Without the camera, he assures me, family, friends, the cow of good conscience. That was my old brain, I explain, but I suppose I can still send a note. He left pen and paper and told me he'd pick them up later.

When Hakim leaves I sit, or watch things grow. Sometimes I do both, my hair for example, it's important I not become idle. While he is here I muster as many words as the situation requires. I don't know if he knows, but I can't connect them to the things that I'm thinking. I will count the stones on the floor, two chairs, state clearly there is only one fork, one spoon and one pail. I checked, that's how I know I don't have a knife in my sock. A list will announce my predicament, things as they are in a letter home, west generally. I drew a map so Hakim would know where to send it, but it's not to scale. I can only see the objects I'm naming and as any trifling philosopher will tell you, that is the whole world.

Texas, I have found all I have lost in a page torn from your almanac. I am telling stories again, a gap and a gathering, this and not that while cities burn. A fruit ripens having already lived. I am born to my departure, born to what is hidden in these spaces where we have never touched, again. There was a life, conjecture broken, vacations earned. I lay down with the elephants. We muddled and ate the morning paper. The details are not important, the details are all there is. Small countries, we softened them for massacre. That's why they don't like me now. Still, there is no precise definition for war; death certainly, dividends, the other, corpses and devotees. Texas can be quite liberal on the subject. A little calibration and we will bestow the disaster. I understand the unattainable, but for this I have not been prepared.

War is full of things you can do with the person next to you, even if he's from Oklahoma. That's because you both speak the same language, the end of perspective. In any case you can't stay awake all the time but if you work together there's a chance you'll outlive him. I was at Harvard when they took New York, deliberating on the question of return and without a trace. The infinite came to mind, a distance now given to the dead. For a moment I knew time as love and falling, silence briefly and later grafted to another failed September. I promised then I would exact my escape by remaining. I was dispatched to interrogate suspects shielding suspects behind suspects without answers. From this room I have informed Texas these people want to kill me because I have oppressed, starved, tortured, exiled and murdered them.

5

The bombs were so loud that my ears hurt for days. In my room time is reported as rupture and loss, point blank and the locus of all meaning. I am the death that waits and calls me to my task – the life of my neighbour because it's too much for one person. Listen, said Aban, you must tell the President what is happening here ... I think he knows ... that's impossible. Texas makes the weapons to stop the weapons that it makes. War is simple, the poor kill each other and trucks bring ammunition and food to the front. Texas always accomplishes what it sets out to do, but it does not know what it has done. Had we been wise, things would not have been different, and stupidity is necessary for knowing things incompletely.

Let's begin the story again. New York swaddled in winter and Victorian brooding, towering Norwegian spruce draped over a vast window, rare birds weather permitting, blue, green, red music while reading Air Force climate reports and nineteenth-century British protectorates' meticulous and extensive documenting of weather and terrain that always delivers the colour of your skin. War was in the air, the assurance of death and suffering of the greatest number for the least cost. A few blood-maddened dogs picking over the ruins. Liberty had cast its net. A new beginning, it looks like the old beginning – the same promises, the same wretched bliss. I wondered if I would miss the snow.

As a diplomat I had recourse to multiple explanations. Appearing and disappearing is the same thing and what I do best. With a slap and a dare I'm in Kabul and Baghdad not to mention the Indian subcontinent, though lately they've been coming around. There are threats everywhere and stockpiles of weapons that do not exist. There is only one nation that can be counted on and situated next to an oilfield. Israel is a very small country, adequate to deliver the technology we make. Peace is possible but war is the mother-lode. We also have a friend in England, that's why we can't step on the Queen, and besides, she might disagree. Texas, Britain and Israel protect us from evil, and this is an axis that actually exists. I'm just hoping the situation doesn't get any funnier.

It is hard to live without madness, emptiness illumined and a thought you can keep. In the colonies people didn't last long, heaped as they were after we'd broken their backs. In 1920 Churchill was the secretary of state for war and for air. He used mustard gas to deal with recalcitrant Arabs and in 1934 David Lloyd George reserved the right to bomb niggers. But the old empires put too many boots on the ground, it was not cost-effective. Every branch, they reasoned, must connect to the tree. Texas prefers clients to colonies, constitutional fictions to keep everything flowing. It knows the shortest distance between two points is a detour. Air power from the Pacific Rim to the Azores in case the strawman-apparent, some two-bit democracy, forgets to mail in the rent.

I am afraid of Buddhist temples above fine restaurants, and the English language. I am afraid for the other man, that I will not be there when he dies. That he will die alone. I am a prisoner and Hakim is my keeper. I don't know if that makes us the same person. I adhere to an obedience that precedes the order. The earth is our deathbed and the moon is no different, me looking at you looking at me. I know how unimportant this is, but there are children torn and scattered on both sides of the wall, sitting ducks that could not see the bombs in their future. They are living inside my head. It is love that gives rise to the other, the earth as a kiss, a splash in the water, blameless like snow, like sleep.

The century is young and Hakim is a patient man. He studies hard, one prisoner at a time. He is not an imam but he gives comfort to a trembling knee. He is here to learn, but first he sees to my comfort. Is the food to your satisfaction … yes it's fine … I can bring more if you like … it is sufficient, but thank you. For his lesson I suggest we not rely on the books left behind. Conversation is best; fragments lost and then lost again. Hakim agrees and he wants to know about Canada. I have cousin there ... I have *a* cousin there ... *I have a cousin there* ... that's right ... thank you brother, what's it like ... it's like Texas with more lakes ... I see ... and more fish ... that makes sense ... but they can't find their past ... the fish ... no the people ... why not ... it's a big country ... that's true ... what happened to the prisoner before me ... we killed him.

Mr. President, Afghanistan is on a lifeline from Pakistan. Cut it. I am waiting for a willing coalition of the way it was. Terror and territory approximately equal in the new economy, dread and rhetoric for better pay. I have a pail and a washcloth. I used to have five bathrooms, two with a view. I'm a prisoner but I am not yet speechless. A parrot will go on talking in an empty room, recite its favourite authors and draw attention to the ones who died of old age. My past is over but I can still learn a bird's humility. Lose postulates, suppositions and sneaking suspicions. I am content with a shot in the dark, hell I prefer it, and I promise never to presume its meaning.

In my room the ceiling is the same as the floor except there are no people on it. This room was ours to take, and so was Vietnam. On every street corner and barstool in Saigon was a wilful sister, or the prom queen who left with the town's hard-on. Hot diggity I'm back in Tennessee. War is tough on our soldiers. In the south we are accustomed to a choking morality but we always find a way around the biology. Texas is more to life than what is true. Behind door number one is everything you'll ever need, and it comes in a tin. In the box next to it are the keys to a new Cadillac. Adventure is what we signed up for, just like Robert De Niro. In quick out quick, man alone, that sort of thing. We can't stop to scrape the girls off the ceiling.

The last century belongs to cowboys and wankers, you can tell them apart by their accent. In Piccadilly, God does not answer for third parties and in Texas every war is a rumour, probably from Sweden. My one plate is clean and so is my spoon. My work is done. From the bed I survey the table and from the table I check the bed. There's no one else here so I must be the one speaking. In the hills of Afghanistan children are no longer afraid of the dark, they are afraid of the Air Force. As for the monster under the bed, he's the mighty nothing, renowned for his desert fighting. When the time comes everyone will leave together and there will be no slow walkers in the event of burning or suffocation.

In New York a squirrel refused to hear my confession and, he said, you are not handsome. I paced to and fro and to the river to ponder his complaint. You will return with tales of perfect metaphor, he mocked. In church they took one look at my hump and withdrew their invitation. I paid a man to listen. I told him I had fine dreams during the war and from behind my desk I rebuilt the German culture. I am acquainted with the period, he said, French restaurants and Hungarian opera, happiness and camps, reckless breeding inside the empire. My deformity is permanent, I said, place a mirror close to my lips and you'll see. He who dies well has died before, he said. Is that it, I asked, or could it be much worse.

We talked about the swagger of an autumn fern, butterflies with a broken wing and some dead animal in the nursery. A mantis preys where a mantis lies. But I had not yet been marked for grief, the long look back. When Texas came to call I renewed my allegiance to hygiene and my interest in science, summers torn by a raging sky that I would soon deliver. I have come to love this desert landscape, a few bloodless branches on a hill throwing meagre roots into their own decay. I serve a master colder than any word, winking from the inside of my condition.

One night, God must have slipped in before Hakim locked the door. I don't know who sent him but I respectfully wrote down his name and filed it with my own in the shoebox I keep under the bed. I had long acquired the habit of recording all coming and going on the assumption that one day my notes would help me to decipher the difference. God said this would probably be a good time to get to know each other since we would soon meet again in eternity. This is no place for small music, I said. I need what time is left and besides, I explained, I have long since begun to live in a world without me.

On the diplomatic front there was not a word out of place. In a letter I wrote to the President I told him that I had located the obvious and was determined to preserve its meaning but I was having difficulty, given my situation, juggling the international agenda. I wrote in detail of my recent meeting with God, his immense head and his hatred for all of mankind. Mr. President, lately I have been thinking about a little property in Texas, next to Prairie Chapel Ranch. I am hoping that you and I can clear a little brush. I am rowing a teacup back to Texas, reporting the name that names nothing, repeating the thing that has just been said. Together we could still look for Jesus, but this time I want a Jesus who thinks.

6

I INVENTED CLARITY. I was building a name, you see.

As to the celestial, the orbital assertions of Galileo, I remain neutral. When I was born the camps had electricity and the trains had already moved the bodies. Those who have all will be forgiven and from those who have little, it will be taken. Birth is a single occasion to the end of time. In a firestorm clothes will sometimes carbonize and keep their shape, the memory of a body missing. I do not know with whose words I am speaking but I am not responsible for everything. I was given a job, kill for the common good, protect the people or was it the brotherhood. I was distracted. God himself, several stories high, moved slowly amongst us. It was a holiday, the streets were closed, cocktails and shopping, life after death. Who could think.

When Aban saw the young man approaching with a gun he knew his part – hired dog. We go through assistants like candy said the soldier who delivered his file to my desk. There are plenty more where he came from. Aban delighted in burning through the Texas cash, but for a modest sum. After the war he would build a house of lemons to kill the stench of paradise. I came here to work, negotiate after the bodies amid deserts red with politics. We were walking twenty kilometres a day, moving toward the perimeter. Words were disappearing in their meaning, objects in the naming. It was a massacre. I scattered Aban's ashes in the desert, crimson with the blood of Texas watching. They will kill me.

Everyone in the Third World loves the Texas dollar. Charity is giving a little of it back to the people we took it from. The poor will learn to sing by singing. Cock a doodle do, cock a doodle don't. In 1957 the Security Council resolved that the bloodshed in Algeria had to stop. France agreed. The way to stop the blood, they reasoned, is to have no more blood to shed. They entrusted the task to civilian militias. Two thousand French citizens volunteered in the first twenty-four hours, they were encouraged to shoot anyone who looked suspicious. I am giving you the numbers as I find them. I will give you some more later. For example, for the next seven years nobody French was charged with killing an Algerian.

Hakim delivered my food in the afternoon and left immediately. See you tomorrow, he said. This is tomorrow and he's late. On the table there's a stack of books, I poach a line or two and spin another list. Come back to me Hakim, without you there's only this. In my room there is a mirror, I check each morning to see that I am in it. I know soon, after the blade finds the narrow between my shoulders and my chin, Hakim will be with me once again. We're going to the same place. Our plan is to return in a few thousand years, after Texas leaves, when the desert yields to a mountain or a spring. Look for us when it finally lifts its wing. I hope I don't forget the name of that dish I liked so much yesterday.

Dread lies just behind the ribcage. It used to be a rumour that sailed from England or from Spain. In 1960 I flew to Guatemala. Everyone on our side was wearing mirrored sunglasses. Mayan farmers were trampling on the rights of landowners. With the right I signed contract after contract, agreement was more difficult on the left. Machine-gunning began at dawn to aid in the negotiations. Law and order right between the eyes. Hakim is back, with a fat lip and one arm bandaged. He makes no apology for his tardiness. You're lucky I come at all ... that's true, what happened ... Texas soldiers ... oh ... last night they took a shortcut through my bedroom ... I'm sorry ... it's not the first time ... were they looking for me ... they didn't say.

If I were a tailor I would have built this prison from blue and yellow fabric and if I were a stonecutter I would be living inside what I have done. Hope is a little bit of thread, a patch of wheat, a peach, things a geologist cannot find. Men with scarred lungs stumble out of mountains, sometimes it's called Egypt and sometimes it's Wyoming. It's just people making things, mostly from dust or dry rot. In forty years or so you'll get off where you got on, the mountain growing inside your chest. God won't be there, he only worked six days and quit. The future is a Buick rusting in the driveway and re-runs of *I Love Lucy*. But it doesn't matter because you realize finally, it's all you ever wanted.

This story has everything except a story, phantom castles, disasters and bordellos, a string of ducks. Cities built to last. To the multitude, the dark and yellow breeds, creeds and tongues, we deliver trinkets and a jumble of dead words. It is important that they know they can be arrested, beaten and starved. In Cuba the CIA failed to poison Castro so they poisoned the crops and livestock instead. Still they could not improve on its investment climate. In 1964 Texas was in Brazil delivering yet another economic miracle. Encouraged by the results we moved on to Paraguay, Nicaragua and Guatemala. On Sundays the children of Afghanistan put firecrackers up the frogs' asses. The frogs have no idea that it's a day of rest but the children know what day it is. It is a day of practice.

Secret prisons are illegal in Texas, so we built them in Poland, Romania, Lithuania, Thailand, Jordan, Egypt, Morocco, Cuba and some other countries that will be disclosed eventually. Vice President Cheney explained to Congress that a successful defence requires that he be empowered to hold and interrogate suspects for as long as necessary and without restriction. The program is called Enhanced Interrogation Techniques and the way it works is that people are arrested for nobody knows why, taken to nobody knows where, to do what nobody knows for as long as it takes. There are jailers who do not speak directly to the accused and others who, before all happiness ends, unload their heads into the prisoner's misfortune. I have been here some time now, or an hour.

The door opens and a man, badly bruised, is thrown into my room in shackles and a hood. The guards leave, I go to him. I cannot unchain his hands but I uncover his head. He inhales deeply. They told me I would be killed, he said, before a camera and a firing squad. I was taken to a courtyard. I tried to refuse a blindfold. The face of my executioner was all I had left. The order, shots, then nothing, I do not know for how long. I heard laughing but there was no pain. Am I dead? I was led back to my cell to die no doubt, more slowly. I could not control my legs or my bladder for days and then I walked a little. What day is it, he asked. Sunday, I said. He had not eaten for days, I fed him what food and water I had. He was not from Texas. I am from the wrong town, he said, what will happen to me … I don't know … I'm just a shopkeeper … have you told them … yes of course, this country is only good for rocks and goats.

When the guards brought me my cellmate it was the middle of the day and I had been sleeping, training for when I would no longer be here. But I do not forget that I am happy. I like the rigour of its speech, its many suits of clothes. I am always the first to arrive, early, as I am expected later, after my annihilation. I moved toward the window, thousands of stars, a crystal ball and then I remembered I had company. It will take both of us to finally say nothing. We will be killed, I said … I know. That evening the shopkeeper was removed from my room still in shackles and a hood. I am alone again and so I must think, a stirring in the first person before succumbing to the impossibility of thought, of the end perhaps, which does not belong to us though we can find ourselves there.

Let's begin again, again. I got a job in New York. The dogs walked by my window on the beach south of Brooklyn and west of Baghdad. Dying, such as it is, I have nothing to say about it, really. The story began arbitrarily, certain of its decision in the plenty of its paralysis. Is a week longer than a week? Let's begin the story on a golf course with the President of Texas watching. He asked if I had been to Harvard. I told him about New York girls and the dog people. Existence is the one we make, he said. The story unfolds in a small Mediterranean town. My father was dreaming about New York, my mother was picking chestnuts and my brother went mad eating sugar and lemons by a freshwater stream. I will never forget, and I will never know.

In December, 1987 all but two member states of the Security Council voted in favour of a resolution to define terrorism. The United States and Israel explained that they could not support the motion because it did not identify, as terrorists, the people who resist their aggression. Honduras abstained. Often I begin my day as a rabbit, some day my ears will find their immensity and then I will begin as an elephant, an elephant in repose. Meanwhile, here is a list of my body parts: these are my legs and this is my chest, this is my back and these are the shoulders that refused me my wings. I keep one foot in my mouth because I can't reach my dick. I walk with a limp, shoulder to shoulder with the dead. Together we will bring up the rear.

Hakim is here and when he's not, there is a murmur adequate to my purpose. I have decided to stay because I cannot do otherwise. He has brought me another book and he wants to schedule his next language lesson. It costs a lot of money to be poor, he said. I told him it's always been that way. He thinks that speaking English will help him find a better job. The poor are not important, I explained, it is the brand that must go on. Goebbels sold National Socialism like Madison Avenue sells toothpaste. The people are the object, a statistic, more or less, at best a detail that creates confusion. They are not the reason for anything. Texas returns words to their source, sounds prior to and stripped of all meaning. Many will starve, the rest is misleading. Hakim has nothing and everything he will have is already spent. He simply cannot afford our ideas.

7

All of my ancestors were alchemists: shoes, teeth and ashes, or whatever else they could lay their hands on. We are adapting well to the future, to every child a gun to run out the luck of the father. In Calabria we sold ribbons to the mayor's wife. I'm not from here, but I have been trained to navigate on glacial lakes. We speak of time as though there were only one way to endure. Outside this room the poor are still selling oysters to the rich. I keep all objections to myself. In Chile the casualties were not recorded as per the usual conventions, injury was logged in a language that has yet to be spoken. When I was there I lived beyond the marshes several miles from the nearest railway station. I was sent to clarify misconceptions about the state – all of this is ours, and so is this.

On the streets of Santiago the secret police shot a folk singer forty-four times. I don't know what kind of car they were driving but the car of choice for Argentinean and Chilean death squads was the Ford Falcon. During labour negotiations in Buenos Aires The Ford Motor Company conceded a one-hour lunch. Union leaders were then taken to a facility within the factory gates and tortured in a room that has never existed, that's why there's no one to get even with. All anyone can do is tell the story. Yesterday's butchers are the good men of tomorrow, and as for the union leaders, we just need stiffer sentences.

My wife and I have been seen and foreseen in our favourite places notating our disapproval. We never missed a Manhattan hootenanny, save for a more reputable affair in Paris or in London. We learned to walk, not here, not there, but among the images. That's her in a hat. In New York bottled water is a lifestyle and we sent money to Guatemala so they could buy back their bananas. We always switched the lights off to save the planet and laughed when we knocked over a chair. We talked endlessly about the future, oodles of words. First she talked about me, then I talked about her. I don't remember a time when there was no sound at all. Watch out for stray fingers, teeth and car bombs on your way to the gym.

The bird has arrived from New York. We first met when he flew into the glass of my Manhattan office and fell not one metre from the windowsill. It will die, I thought. Behind it was a drop of four stories to a garden in full bloom, from its half-opened beak a fluid the colour of wine. Be quiet, he said, words will speak of cherry blossoms and still ruin a perfect death. Then he hopped with difficulty to lie at some distance from me. I took no pleasure in his suffering and continued to work calmly, glancing occasionally in his direction from my side of the glass, the same glass that, for the bird, didn't exist even after he hit it. He turned and faced the garden. To his credit he did not diminish a single flower by mentioning its name.

The bird had flown thousands of miles and was now perched on the windowsill of my prison cell. A small aperture that, but for my size and lack of wings, apparently opens onto Texas. He took a look around, flew onto the kitchen counter and then onto the table. You've come a long way bird … you've no idea … oh … hawks on the eastern seaboard, flying fish in the Atlantic and wild bees in Africa … it sounds terrible … not to speak of the desert … how did you find this place … via satellite … are you in contact with Texas … yes of course … do they know where I am … no … but you are here … yes … you can tell them where I am … that won't be possible … why not … dead birds don't talk.

It seems I have been abandoned to a room identical to the one I am in. I curse the sun for the misery it brings only once. Listen. A few thousand years ago it was clear that no one would ever know what happened here. Seek faith in the fragments of a name, in the scent of a dream. Something of the invisible will be returned to you from the inside of an apricot. We were wrong to praise God, our crops have never been his concern. We wrote letters from the trenches, sought glory in a turtle shell. We always give more than He will admit to taking. The bird was now pacing the length of the table. What about my work, bird … what about it … it's not finished … nothing could be more trivial … I see … you have a rule for every absence, and everywhere you bring the law.

In 1958 I was walking through Central Park on my way home from the zoo. I stopped to talk to a man on a bench. I killed him, or maybe he died in a Broadway play. What's important is that I felt the knife as it penetrated his ribs. New York is gaining momentum from two broken towers, thousands of miles of twisted steel, snakes with Manhattan money to dispense the truth loud and clear. When was it not like this. We are ready to decide what we have already done. There's never been a bad time to dismantle a nation. My job was to plan yesterday's murders and adjust accordingly our date of arrival. Between postings I renewed my interest in theatre and organic food.

I'm tired, said the bird, I will give you your instructions later … what instructions … don't ask questions … why not … there are no answers ... are you sure ... these are your words not mine … that's true. Texas, when I die all of my beginnings will end. Deny everything. These ramblings are but a dull spade in the hands of a muddled gardener. Say something about history and move on. The people will believe you, they are not expecting to win. You and I have tasted oysters; another time, a different mind and I will have reversed the tale. I am nothing if I cannot defeat the story I make. A few hours in your mouth and I can shove these images up my ass. Texas, you know what to do.

Hakim brings me magazines, newspapers and sometimes books left behind by diplomats and soldiers who are no longer at large. He is an enthusiastic student and points to the words he can identify. I notice that the bird is watching us from behind an empty planter next to the fireplace. I become flustered though I cannot say why. I can hardly be held responsible for things that do not exist. But just in case, I decide to feel Hakim out on the subject, hypothetically of course. I'm sure you have seen by now, I begin, that I was born small and for the most part I have remained unemployed. But if things should go from black to grey or the other way around, in short a glimmer or a wink, after the names are revoked, in your opinion would anyone, God for example, when operating in plain view, understand me. No, said Hakim.

Before Hakim walked out the door he said he would refuse to live in a world without God. Hakim lives, therefore God, proof finally that my life will go on. I'll have to give up my six-and-a-half rooms in the sky. Building, I think, is much more expensive when it's layered in the opposite direction. Hakim has been with me for weeks now, or I just arrived. Every time he tries to tell me how long I've been here I put a finger in each ear. It's important I lose all sense of time. A moment here is longer than eternity elsewhere, I explain, and life in this room is immense, larger than it's ever been. Hakim pulls a tiny calendar from his pocket and we guess at the day when I'll know such things for sure.

Idiot, said the bird after he heard the door lock … I found Hakim's reasoning quite sound … I'm talking about you … I see ... all that crap about eternity ... you're dead ... so ... you came back ... I live in your head ... your point ... I ask the questions ... I see ... well ... well what ... have you anything to report ... I don't think so ... that doesn't surprise me ... why are you here, bird … I was sent by the Pentagon … what for … to institute a program of re-education … you can do that … I worked in Hollywood … I see … from time to time it will be necessary to lecture whoever is present … what do you mean whoever is present ... there will be others … I see … the war has not been going well … I agree … our intentions are coming under suspicion … what are our intentions … that's classified … did you have a good rest … no ... oh ... I'm having trouble adjusting to the time change.

The bird began to pace the length of the table. In New York I told you to wait, that the sun would dry my carcass and the rain wash away the stain … I was called, bird … you were not needed … how do you know … I died on an asphalt roof that was too remote for the remains to be swept up with the garbage ... I see ... my death belongs to you now ... I want my own ... try to make the best of it ... what should I do ... wait ... why don't we leave this place ... don't be ridiculous ... a small town in Italy or France perhaps, where instead of changing their skin they put on a little more lipstick ... I don't exist and you're under contract ... you said I'm not needed ... that has nothing to do with it ... they are going to kill me ... we have a contingency for that.

His pacing became more agitated and more certain. I feel a speech coming on ... really ... pay attention ... ok. He took a few deep breaths and from the edge of the table he spoke to the great unwashed, Mussolini, before he was hanged. Our President is at war, prescriptively and descriptively steadfast by absence of variant to preserve the purpose of nature, nation and asset ... what ... don't interrupt ... sorry ... ours is to communicate to those who are absent and independent of the actuality of our intention after a death that moreover belongs to a structure not to be examined and developed in the manner as continuous modification and progressive extenuation of presence, representation and above all articulation of the mark that we abandon as elsewhere and deliver without interpretation.

Keep going.

... If we speak of the President in reference to any question, a condition to which he answers not at all in defence of statutes as the first principle of apparatus and trembling, we are the substance and the subject of his increasing, but we serve as praxis. In Texas anyone can be President designate and distinct from those who suffer. Our existence can only emerge at a distance from the deduction in the contingency of its position and though I, like you, truly do not know what this means, it is here that we shall be tagged and tallied. The President will withstand the cost of denial as mouth and signature, interchangeable and very democratic.

Got it ... I'm not sure ... everything I say is important ... it sure sounds like it, I regret you flew into my window in New York ... birds can't see glass ... oh ... if you put stickers on it, it helps ... I see ... that's why I died ... oh ... there were no stickers ... I'm sorry ... there is a lot of glass in Manhattan ... that's true ... it was hell ... I can't imagine.

From now on the bird would be wherever I looked, in profile, because he didn't want history to find him boring. He was dead, and he flew in from New York, this I could not have predicted. I can only assume his absence was too hard for me to swallow. Was he friend or foe, or was he boring? All these questions made me tired. The bird watched me cross the room and lie on the bed. Have you met the President, he asked ... I'd like to say yes.

As a diplomat I was present and absent for all executive speeches. In Texas Bucharest USA we agreed with a persistent President leaning toward merger and saying to a sea of hungry faces that Ethiopia is in Rome, Pakistan is in London and moneyed Muslims were pricing Parisian condos. In a cold and pelting rain he stated clearly that dictators make good capitalists but must be opposed, after they're dead. Atrocity is opportunity he said with even less clarity. Then he asked everyone to sign a document that was making the rounds as he spoke. It was the list that would help us decide what to do with the scraps. There were so many important things that he needed to say to us. Prosperity, prosperity and prosperity.

8

Behind every border there are countless addresses but God favours the madman who sits in the palace. It takes an army to spread truth and justice. Before I left the Capital the President assured me that just wars were making a comeback and for us there's no other kind. That's why I was dispatched to this country. Why every day I sat with Aban on plastic chairs in the heat, with a fixed concrete table between us. There was a generator and an old air conditioner inside, but then we could not hear ourselves talk. The mornings were reserved for civic councils, what remained of the politics in this tortured country. As a rule Aban recommended that these groups be refused. Slaves built the pyramids, he said, fuck the politicians.

At lunchtime Aban told the soldiers who kept the perimeter that we were not to be disturbed. The people were kept at a distance designed to keep us, me mostly, safe from improvised explosives. But he couldn't do anything about the airplanes that flew overhead. We ate and talked while a line of people stood in the sun. Aban told his friends not to poison my food. I, in turn, took no interest in what he did with the money. War is compromise, peace more so. After lunch people were let in, first a father with a little girl on his shoulders. The cashbox was in plain view and just out of reach from the other side of the table. Everything needs replacing, the father explained, and we don't have enough to eat. Aban handed him a handful of bills. Don't forget who gave it to you, he said, this war won't last forever.

In an air raid every basement is a potential tomb and every street a crater. You can run, but don't try to understand the impulse. Choose any direction. Aban and I took cover beneath the concrete table. When the sky cleared the little girl lay in her father's arms and before she succumbed to bits of glass and shrapnel she assured him that a foot is not a bee. It is good to be a bee, she said, but a foot lives in a shoe and cannot fly away. At the funeral her small body was shrouded in linen and carefully loaded into the back of a pickup truck. Behind the truck was her family, a gap to respect the mourners, and then a group of young men, boys mostly with steel pipes and sticks. Texas prohibits the carrying of automatic weapons.

Her father took her everywhere, Aban told me later, to protect her. At the dawn of aviation the reporting of air attacks included the names of the firms that produced the airplanes. Solidarity is how unions overcame steel. Overcoming is a word susceptible to debt and trembling. Everything dead in our survival, nothing left to do but start a tab of staggering admission. Texas is the future, the future is death. Money does not talk but it does walk. New York has money, style and the imbecility of positive thinking. The next day a car outfitted with loud speakers circled the streets, a voice boomed. In war the dead decide events.

I was born with a tongue that will not speak ceaselessly and says I. I spit, choke and fuck this war. Progress is impossible and pursued with a vengeance. Armies give way to livers, red then bluish and after so many tears, nothing. Everything was waiting for me in this room and everybody that comes here talks about me, aloud. There is a chair where I sit to put on my socks. I have to stand to put on my pants. This story was stretched out on the floor with one eye on the door and looking to me for asylum. The little girl in the air raid is without language with which to discard her affliction. She is leading us in a memory that allows us to live in our collapse. She is fixing the unknown, ruined words that will not wait for that which cannot be done. She is only, when she is no longer.

Texas, we met at Harvard. I was drunk on a Tuesday morning, basking in my American suicide. You made me an offer I just couldn't refuse. I was set on a plan prepared so many years ago in coffee houses where we scripted songs to dead poets and a lost war. I was working day and night to topple a comma and a noun. A thought, a grain of sand will fell a government but the order never came. A soldier, you said, sets in motion what the executive will deliver. It's vaudeville, the old bait and switch, and the archive is a record of things we'll decide later. A mystery, because it never happens here.

I accepted your offer, of course, and abandoned my plans to burn Boston. Then you spoke to me of an alleged elsewhere, of work that leaves its mark in places it has never been. In any case, you explained, it's not up to you.

Texas, what exactly is the matter here? Why can't we turn the lights back on and why must everyone be hungry for our plan to work? You have explained it, but in this room I forget. A conveyer belt of embedded proponents, shrink-wrapped billions and a cake for emissary Bremer, the viceroy with two books and a box of raisin bran in khaki boots dry-cleaned up to his neck in a theory that works best when it all goes wrong. Open markets unleashed without irony by veterans of the corner office waging pre-emptive war on a people relieved to be merely dispossessed of all they have. Rumsfeld said that it's over but for a few fanatics, well hidden. What he meant is that it's over in Miami, and on Wall Street it grows smaller in meaning.

This room is ten paces wide and twelve paces long, exactly. There is a beam that spans the length, pine I think. I am examining the worm and the hook, the moon is where I put it but something has gone terribly wrong. The voice I hear is my own but that doesn't make this a prayer so it must be just another list. What is certain is that I'm not finished so I can't be obliterated. Hell, Texas, I never even made an appointment. I follow the chatter between these walls like a squirrel from room to branch in the hope of losing all the names. Hakim brings me something agreeable to eat, sustenance so I can work. I examine charter and rumour, rapture and sodomy, dread begets murder in your magnificent churches. I found you, Texas. The dead are dead forever and when we are, we are not here.

Bury us deep, Texas, and pray for us in our time of killing. We are driving the wrong way with whisky and a song that will not reach the future. Texas, what did you do on those nights when the mirror was bare? Did you dream? Of coloured lights and endless tits, Asian children with fingers in monkey heat, working to fill the shelves between the thighs of

Christian women sleepwalking through your suburbs. When I am with you I lose all memory of things burning. I stroll instead through fields of poppies vanishing into a morning dust. Everyone agrees this is not the last word on a massacre. When things are no longer Wall Street reports like ants on a bone.

I am not afraid of death, it's just that I don't think my eyes will adjust and there's no place to hide in the dark. The city where I am held captive is the same as New York except New York has more banks, and there Arabs are still driving Mercedes. In Arizona people can't enjoy their termite-infested porches. There is dust in their mouths, an ache in their bed and some tribe the size of smoke is amassing at the Mexican border. Just in time the President is reporting pyramids the size of money, where we dream disaster in gutted hospitals full of people dying alone like martyred sparrows on a garbage heap. A slow night and sleep you can almost touch as it stops breathing.

I cannot leave this room but from a distance I can see myself in it so I must be in California. In California the sun sets behind the ocean and one star lights the sky for the next, and there I am, sitting on the veranda. I think I'm developing a taste for the universe. Watch out for the mouse said the bird ... what mouse ... when he comes you will know. Planets fall. Here and there a city raises a noon march past the five and dime. The girl from Fenton, Louisiana plucks a rose for the soldier atop the machine. She is looking for the dusk and the dawn, for him it is enough to touch a satin dress, a birth and a funeral in a town that will dream them both on the instalment plan.

Cockfuck, poets everywhere are haunted by the insufficiency of the word's absence. I have two bowls and a pail. Enter Hakim in the early morning. I thought you were someone else, I said ... really, I said. He has brought me a real fork and a spoon. If the guards find it, he says holding up the fork, tell them it was already here ... what about the spoon ... it's fine. I will minister my utensils, timing is the key. My room is on the wing of a blizzard, inside all is still. I have never seen the storm. Talk acquiesces to the assurance that nothing is said. I promise. I will ask to wait and say all when all is missing. I am the accused. I lied about how I got here, I lied about who I am and I am lying now. Interior monologue is a literary device. Outside this window is the best part of the inside of my room.

Texas, I'll get back to you when you are no longer here. I'm charmed by your homicidal will, your love affair with murder. How you tickle the west and dangle the east on a string. Some places you say are better than others, Houston or Dallas where memory has not had occasion to ripen, heads with bigger holes than Swiss cheese. We do not possess the object we take by naming but we are returned to it when it is not there. If I say that I have a gun, what I mean is I do not have a gun. The thing is averted. This is history. When Hakim leaves the room I am released to gather the infinite. Death will find me where I am no longer. In the time of time absent history consents to atrocity, it does not take place. Nothing is older than the moment stirring. November 9, 91 BC, is missing.

9

The story, again, New York, Texas. The dog people line the streets with means and plenty of style, protect the camera from the poor and oppressed. Loud and clear opportunity, democracy as the agenda of a tiny huddle and the muddle we're in. You have to keep somebody out, said Andy to his mopey son Opie, or it wouldn't be a club. The whole of the scary outside cancelled, that's how everybody knows that we won. On Broadway I dined with Greenspan on Labrador trout and white wine. Make sure, he told the chef, that everyone knows there's not enough to go around. We have plans for the poor, he explained. Land is just too expensive and when there's no room left, we'll stack them. Money is promised and its lack distracts them to the day they die. In Mayberry they think they can still make ends meet but in Detroit the body is truth, mute and assembling at the end of the line.

The rich will still prosper after they're dead, they've made provisions. They know nothing is more dangerous than living. Hakim has entered my room with an air of benevolence, a measure of conscience and malice. Today is the day I walk in the courtyard where the guards play cards and park cars. A small garrison is stationed in this mansion that should be in Scotland. Hakim said that I am an important prisoner. The video he took of my arrival is on every channel so why kill the star, I reasoned. I asked him to keep an eye on the ratings. I hope they don't slip, though all there was to lose was lost long before I joined the academy. This might be a good time to mention that in my situation the first thing to go is the cranium. Still I live and die by the numbers, that's how I know I'm an artist. It's a gift, nothing really, and nothing is still just arithmetic.

Hakim and I are going out to the courtyard. I hope he remembers to bring me back in. Before leaving my room I am shackled, because we are expecting a visitor, he explains. We have our secrets. Outside a few vines are still twisting in the sun, in and out of grey and splintered lattice. In this town all the drains have been blown out of the ground. Discarded water from the kitchen is diverted through pieces of broken pipe and finds its way to the little bit of green that garnishes the house. I wonder who's watering my plants in New York. Hakim says I should avoid such thoughts. On the other side of the wall is the crest of three palm trees. Electricity is available for a few chance hours a day and water from an old well next to the house. On the whole Bechtel is not delivering on its promise. They are still new to the region, Hakim explains, the situation is complicated and then there's the war. That's true, I said.

Hakim is still pondering the miracle and scale of the Texas enterprise. From the courtyard we can hear, through an open window, a chorus of men inside the house. They are agitated but not with each other. A representative is arriving to recruit for a militia from which, apparently, few will return. The men stationed to this house are looking for ways to explain themselves as immovable. I asked Hakim if he could be chosen and taken away with the others. I am not a soldier, he said, and my proficiency in languages is essential to the mission here. I was the only prisoner and fluent in his tongue but this sort of reasoning is not useful. To my surprise I was allowed to continue pacing the perimeter of the courtyard while the guards and the visiting envoy, a thin nervous man, negotiated my fate. Kill him. We can't. Why not? He's on television.

I am already what I will be later. I know where I'll be killed and soon I'll know when. The comedy is in the details, my unravelling as described by commentators and analysts who cannot agree on hell or high water. This house was built by an Englishman and if you believe that, a bird said there's a mouse on the way. Still, this is not what I wanted, a confession and a bicycle rusting in the places it has never been. You and I no longer separate, merely impossible, we endure. Who closer? A little further and we shall be what is not yet, if that be seeing. Such landscapes are previous to the light. That brush sees a question that is not here yet. The trees in the frame do not exist yet they are still green. The horse and the bird still gallop and fly. There was flying before birds. There was flying before flying.

Night follows day, not as foil but another light before the day breaking. The sacred sleeps on broken glass, eyes open and opening with each and every scar. Waiting makes the future possible. By this absence God will find his place among the living, matching nearly a poet's love, nature's naming. What is the song if not persistence and before any beginning. Everywhere madness waits in darkened doorways and in basements, for Kesey's pillow blessing. It speaks but not to us, it speaks so that it will not lose itself. History is the same mistake, one war and then the next to keep the corners lit. No return without our say so, no land without consent.

Sorry for the invasion, the people dead and burning in the street. I have lived so little and that is why I speak. Each morning I went to work, seldom screamed and never hit my head against the wall. I lived in America, bourbon and neckties, the best minds, Moloch in a padded cell. I have deciphered nothing and so I have asked Hakim for a dog, something that would look at me and know. He said it's not practical. The rich are worth more than the poor and murder has never been forbidden, though it does not call our name. In Texas streams flow under wooden bridges and grasses are watered twice a week. Children set out for places they can't pronounce to strike a blow for freedom, or free enterprise. It's easy to mix them up but it doesn't matter, both are worth killing for.

In Texas a nickel will get you a dime's worth and the nickel you save goes into a brand new bank account. Darkness is the wrath of Texas, terror is its frozen breath. Hakim ushered me in from the courtyard and removed my shackles. It's just us now. The men stationed to this house were loaded into a truck and taken away to the war. First there is nothing and then there is nothing forever. That's why I never take photographs in Paris. The first optic laws were observed by Aristotle in 330 BC. In 1000 AD the ideas were picked up by the Persians and by 1839 England had its first camera. In Rome I built cathedrals, and before the advent of the English tourist I tore them down again.

In the nineteenth century the opium trade was the mainstay of the empire. I sailed to and from the orient to protect the Queen's interest. Each time I returned, it put an end to my wife's longing and so she left with the Queen's photographer, shortly after he'd been invented. All she took was a parasol and a lawn chair, a spoonful of sand. In a note she wrote life is short and that she would never write again. She sent pictures. I keep them in the shoebox underneath my bed. I went looking for the things that had already happened, the same old stone to roll. I never learn, the words to stem the flood are the words I throw away. That's why these lines keep on disappearing.

Sometimes I speak for Texas and I know that we are winning, but from this room it's hard to tell. I have consented to the fall, but not the splat. The truth is no more, and less than a shrug. In my opinion, you can't trust anybody that isn't trapped under a bus or a building. All of this makes my disappearing difficult, and disappearing is all I know. Texas has asked that I keep a running tally of the dying but I will refuse to report my own. Death is simply the result, the more practical side of my enterprise and apparently, God's work. Everybody knows about his day of rest but what about the other six. When I came to this country I knew his reputation but I was dazzled nonetheless. This region was once the centre of the universe, the stories pile up and one God cancels the next. I can't wait to meet the one that I'll invent.

There are lines sharper than a blade to stab you in the brain. The scribblers on Madison Avenue are delivering on their promise. This is how the republic was made permanent. They will take you from a soiled rug in Jersey to the Riviera in just a few frames. Hollywood is assuming the work of civilization. The white man had his burden and death camps were a good idea but the war to end all wars is at nine Eastern, six Pacific. Please take a seat. The stars are shining bright, blondes, redheads and brunettes. Bogart early out of the trenches will teach us how to imitate an opinion. We are all in the picture now, eating the right bowl of cereal from a busted couch in Appalachia. Death is all around us but we can't smell it. That's because of the glass, and the corpses are all wearing makeup.

10

For several nights I heard and observed a mouse as he peeked in and out from behind some loose stones next to the fireplace. He was a foolish little mammal who took great pleasure in losing and then finding himself on the return of an uncertain spiral. A promiscuous salutation in and out of the present that entertained him to no end, as he left once again to prepare for his next entrance. I assumed it was the bombs that drove him indoors. The weather here is not hostile to rodents and for the moment there was little else to explain his arrival. Then I remembered the bird's counsel, watch out for the mouse. But the creature was perfectly what one might expect, in short, a mouse. Still, I thought it best to exercise restraint. I would delay my decision to feed it or kill it.

During these early days I noticed a method to his coming and his going, a pattern. He was learning my habits. This was a rodent who knew the world and its ways. It was not yet clear if he could speak. The bird, by contrast, being dead, tended to get to the point. Perhaps the mouse was a plant, here to record nouns and their suffixes before the approaching speechlessness, the day when I and all twenty-six characters drown in a thimble. Admittedly a change for the better, but a loss nonetheless, and my other trip to the wilderness. I don't remember the first because I wasn't born yet, and I'm still waiting for the second. I hope there's a lake and fancy clothes from Paris or London without all the civilization. Or nothing, at ten times the size.

The truth is I don't know what's on the other side of the door, but every day I do the work so that it will open tomorrow. I am disguised as a Texas diplomat in a potato patch. I am of this world and others as well. I pace day and night but you'd never know it from the stones that make up the floor. I walk barefoot, through mountains and dry riverbeds. What I've learned is that a stone, marked or unmarked, is not the record of anything. Any place any form is the norm, and at no one's insistence since nonexistence is already its nature. After death comes an abundance of stones. A temple in Jerusalem or opposite the security wall in a heap. There are stones everywhere, but what I'm talking about is the olive tree that was bulldozed from this scene.

Alfred Nobel was the father of dynamite. I have strapped to my back all I can carry and I'm ready to explode all explanation. There are prizes for that now, thanks to Alfred. I want the one for mathematics. That's why I keep this list and the universe too I can explain, since by my calculation it's been here for just a few minutes. Close to the end is where we come in. I see everything with the eyes of a clown. Soon I will die but I am talking here of other things, missing roots, running water, smoke. At the end of this phrase there is no reason dangling, there is no mountain peak. When the door finally opens I will go to the tropics and wait for snow. I remember what is left of a plan hatched with the President and revised by a bird who disagrees with a mouse. We will not speak of the fly we will not speak of.

I overheard you talking to the bird, said the mouse. I had recently lost the habit of consecutive thinking, this is work on a string that is lost and then lost again in a thought that never arrives. The mouse, to say the least, was an interruption. The bird told me about you, I said … the bird is a pompous ass … what are you doing here mouse … I have come to help you finish … finish what … dying … is that necessary … your endeavour is simple to the point of stupidity … what endeavour … you cannot find inside ruin an explanation you exalt to destroy … I see … it's a string of happy chances, a game for you and the bird … happy, that's a strange word for a rodent … no it isn't … what do you know of falling … it's not a destination … then we cannot speak … obviously … what makes you wise, mouse … I live in dirt.

I used to live in a city but I can't remember the name of the country. It's where I told you everything but I'll tell you again. There is life in old photographs, always the same new dress and a ribbon for your hair only. What is proclaimed of the dead is a fiction told for a pot of jam. On earth, children will outwit time with a scoop and a pail while salvation waits. God created the living but it's up to us to annihilate them. Terrorists are who we say they are. We need them in Baghdad and in Paris. The committee to re-elect the President will decide when to reveal their identity. After I die I will come back, and if the ratings are any indication, they will need me to bring in the vote. Every night I climb into the frame having perfected my technique, forgotten by morning as I wash the blood from my skin. A drop of light and a bit of earth is all this story needs, but surely you can see how I'm failing.

Words are no worse than the usual disaster, it is best if we try to go on. This morning someone calling himself the administrator sent me a message from Microsoft, apparently. He said Texas was undeliverable. The book or the movie, I asked. No response. How does he know? This is not a glass of milk or a pickled onion, something he's tasted before. I am inside the space outside my speaking. In any case there is no choice to make, someone should tell the Buddhists. Still, I have everything I need, a fork, a spoon, a plate and a mirror in which to see my reflection. The light too is sufficient. I have explained to Hakim that on Broadway they don't kill the narrator. Go now, I said, and tell the executioner.

If not for the gun at my head I would never have come here. I take to confined spaces poorly and the guards have no respect for the superpower I represent. It, they claim, is the problem and why they will kill me. They are focused, Hakim explained, and so cannot subscribe to more than one point of view. On the West Bank Palestinian families are allotted eighty-three cubic metres of water per annum. Exhaustion set in the moment I signed the agreement. Not everything has to be solved now, is how I pitched it to the Israelis. I have no work and four sons, a father once told me, let them fight and die, it will help them to forget their hunger. What I am telling you now is as plain as a dream. All of this will end in clear waters, a snake and a rattle, bodies broken on a Texas ranch.

Of every living thing I know nothing. My scorn grows smaller as I arrange the lines to this song. A flower comma followed by the slap of a cannon. I am in this room by a thread. Upon my son I have bestowed a life of pain. I am trying to describe the world as I remember it. I don't think I will be getting any more letters. As planes flew into buildings New Yorkers stood united on the banks of dying rivers. Towers are a problem, slow to go up and quick to come down. Soon things would get much worse. Neither Texas nor its managers have the ability to reinvent yesterday's calamity, death and a milkshake. When we finally sent in our soldiers they parked in Africa so as not to stir the attention of those who would soon go missing.

In Texas they say that those who believe in angels will rise and have access to their investments. Before I left Manhattan I made lists, matched my plants to my friends. I had no pets but I was tired of several dogs in the neighbourhood. I had read Albee's definitive work on how to kill a dog with kindness, and then just kill it. His own attempts were unsuccessful so I doubled the dosage. I was adjusting the formula when the Texas messengers walked into my office. War ruins everything. The last item on my list was to instruct my accountant. I am familiar with every loophole, he said, leave it all to me. I asked the mouse for his thoughts, if he himself had found something more permanent than the future. It depends ... on what ... which future ... there's more than one ... there is the one you're asking about and another one ... tell me about the other one ... you can't get there from here.

I will fly away after I die, hallelujah, by and by. This morning I re-measured the beam that spans this room, length and height. I will test its strength with a rope. Hakim says that my plan is no different than the one already in place. My executioner, he assures me, will be mercifully quick. I believe him and remind him that my end is all I have left, my last chance to live. Besides, I confide, I suspect the bird has had a hand in all this … what bird … and he does it for pay … if you want to talk about birds let's talk about the ones we can both see … seeing it won't change anything ... really ... the bird is a bird, and what it's not. Hakim is puzzled by this line of reasoning. I could explain, I explain, but who would explain the explanation.

I am frantic as a moth in this, my last run at the light. Hakim is where his brain meets the air, there, where his country is ending. His stories are always the same. The day was like any other, he lived with his son next to a wall topped with barbed wire. The guards waited safely in their nest and watched young men try to jump over, fall, when the volts hit their pants. Hakim screamed, I guess he thought it was just a bad dream. This is how every story begins, with his dead son, but soon he comes round to politics or philosophy and the poets of this great nation. He is looking for something bigger than an ache. Telling is how we finish things off, how we live with and against our condition. The best listeners are people who are in the same room, more or less. I lie on my back, close my eyes and he talks to another.

Yesterday was our golden age, Hakim begins, the payroll arrived in a black car, a man in a bowler hat like clockwork at the end of each week. Workers made wealth out of smoke, they traded their lungs for a meal. Each night there was a handful of food and plenty of beer. At the factory gate a swarm hoping to work the next shift. People still died, he recalled, but much slower. There was always enough time to say goodbye. This was the beginning of the modern world, I explain. Toilets and telephones, English boots in the Sinai and Leopold in the Congo, who eventually stopped killing Africans for crimes they knew nothing about. Who is Leopold … he was the king of Belgium … I see. It's time for me to go, said Hakim, tomorrow you will tell me more about the king of Belgium … yes of course, I will consult my notes ... what notes ... they're in New York ... I see.

Enter the bird in the robes of a judge. Is this my trial, I ask … your trial ended before you arrived and the verdict was announced before it began … but I had no say … you were represented … by whom … an attorney … what was the outcome … he never capitulated but he died drafting his summation … perhaps we should start again … I don't see the point … I find this conversation very distressing … this is not a conversation … oh … it's more of a sneeze … really … or a note from Switzerland … I see … they make time there … yes of course … it began with a thought … I thought so … then it got stuck … oh … like a Singer sewing machine … I see … or that painting of a horse galloping toward a locomotive … interesting … the outcome is always the same … one would assume … they never collide.

I still send every word back to Texas, apparently they are still needed there, especially in small towns where everybody eats the same thing. I am reporting on Hakim and Aban, the bird and the mouse, books I've not read, matchboxes dampened by rain, children and throwaway cats. Notwithstanding all this, I've not lost my appetite. A prisoner must eat and by all indications I still have a job. The Texas messengers come and go, they review my reports and update the mission. The documents are for the President, I explain, and I wish to complain about the bird … what bird … he's from New York … oh … he refuses to disclose the outcome of my trial … we can't discuss that … why not … we don't have the clearance … it would be useful to know … know what … the results … of what … my trial … are you sure it took place … the bird said it did … the bird that doesn't exist … that's right.

11

ART IS A WORD. DEATH is a word too but that's where I draw the line. I want to be born again, called to direct the affairs of the nation from a two-storey colonial on a cul-de-sac in Virginia. In Orlando Jesus drives a Beamer, in Manhattan he dresses in drag, in Miami he's an assassin. The afterlife has to start somewhere, be it an ambulance or a ditch. In Florida the coroners are punctual but nothing else adds up, old people forget and ballots go missing. Only the TV keeps on blinking and the people must choose between elections and golden oldies. That's how we delivered the presidency, the governor explained, he's the President's brother, a space in between. In Florida there's always a last word, he said, and after that, plenty of chatter.

Not everyone in the coalition sleeps in the kingdom, not all will be saved. Doug Coe is Jesus' secret ambassador. He's in the who's who of the world. As any general from Managua to Mogadishu will tell you, Doug decides and fixes the door when it's squeaking. He tells Presidents when to pray and when to pull the trigger. From El Salvador he brought Generals Casanova and Martinez to the White House. Casanova was later convicted of torture and the CIA disagreed with Martinez so they killed him. Then Reagan increased aid to the death squads by a factor of twenty. Death squads are underappreciated in New York but they are indispensable to the empire. They remind us that death is trivial.

A saintly man, so goes the tale, no longer arrives on a donkey, but the trail is still blood and piss. Doug Coe handpicks one candidate to usher in the new order, his work will be clear in Honduras but it won't make the news cycle. What we don't know is useful as a threat elsewhere. That's how we know that Doug's been around. We just can't find him to praise him. Latin America is not far from San Diego. East on Eight to the Eighty-five then south to Guatemala, but you'll never find it on a school desk in Wichita. Here's hoping for a fall, a crack in the message so the good people of Kansas can see what they're missing. Latin America is no longer a problem and we don't need the farmers anymore except for a few weeks each year, during harvest. At all other times they can live as they please and alcohol will keep them from going insane.

I am not the man who began all of this, that man did not talk to birds. He toiled in the dry light of reason. He had a wife, a son, a job, the man who began at the beginning is dead. While he was sleeping I put a splinter in his eye, while he slept the cold wind blew. I have decided to have myself bronzed so the bruises don't show. The infinite scares me but this room keeps me pinned, I'm just trying to get rid of the death that is pending. Decapitating a man or a chicken is the same thing except the chicken wouldn't presume to know what was happening. The whole world fits in this room, it comes in through the cracks and the window. Yesterday a fly arrived from New York. How is the Big Apple, I asked, tell me, has anything changed. I don't know, he said, I just flew.

I turned that fly into an absence, a no-legged pronoun.

Never again are words to shove up your ass or trade for a stale crust of bread. There is always a there and a when. A knock on the door just before the train leaves the station. It seems the world no longer has room for you. Don't look back, the past is not there anymore. This is the great metamorphosis, it takes place in a room full of new naked friends. Let's agree that we cannot see. Pick up a rusty nail and scratch your name in that chair and someday you will get out of this place, a flea market in Cardiff, a garage sale in Brooklyn or just languishing in a Polish swamp. Don't worry, you're not missing anything. In Warsaw they were on the verge of starvation and eating the children was just a proposal that we were swift to abandon. It just wouldn't work on the continent. To complicate matters, frying pans are only being used to ward off the looters and there are fewer and fewer buildings to cook in.

What is important between us is the third-person singular, our shirts buttoned up. Aban had been shot before, the lead was growing inside him like an old screw. That was the day I survived, he said, death took a look around and – not a word. The Geneva Convention protects people under occupation from torture, illegal detention, the demolition of houses, humiliation and degradation. It denies all claims to territory and resources. It facilitates the withdrawal of the occupier at the end of hostilities. It states that his presence must not become permanent. In 1971, Israel's attorney general, Meir Shamgar, argued that the Geneva Convention was the law in Palestine and hence its transgression. There was no sovereign in 1948 and so there could be no occupation. When something is missing the problem becomes the solution.

In the ghetto I was a soldier's soldier until they attacked from the east and the west and then I eloped with the railwayman's daughter. By way of explanation, she put one hand on my cock and one in my pocket, and for a while we fooled the officials. When Poland crumbled we moved to France. Perhaps there, we thought, there was still room to breathe, though breathing, we knew from living in Warsaw, is not very important. When it was hot we went to the beach, no one enjoys life like the French. At the beach there is always one man in an overcoat. He carries his life in a bag and his lunch in his pocket. He keeps his one good eye on the government. I asked him why he does what he does. He said what he does he does for no reason, and that I should go drown in the ocean.

I'm living in a room that I just can't get to, yet the bird and the mouse come and go. At the beginning of the twenty-first century I was called to the Capital. In Louisiana, hurricanes were gaining on missing wetlands and people were baking on rooftops and bridges. In New York buildings were twisting in plain view. We have pictures. In a crisis everyone settles for less. We met over prayers in Washington, or was it Arlington, to strengthen the chain of command. God was there, so were Doug Coe and the President. God spoke only to Doug. Don't write anything down, he said, and keep the prisoners offshore. Do this right and the war will go on. For my part I can produce a crop of new corpses. Then Doug and the President agreed on the future of some familiar and not so familiar places.

Priests wear black and were the first to write down their ideas. When Moses tried to escape in a basket they pulled him back in. I was there. Later, from under an apple tree I traced a hammer and sickle. I thought they'd come in handy some day. Later I followed the music of bugles to men on horses hunting foxes with hounds, a strange mix of mediocrity and terror. This was the pinnacle of civilization. I guess that's why I needed the hammer. I try not to despair, soon it will end and endings do not require our attention. I know because I'm facing my own execution and thinking is not well suited to the situation. All I can do is wait. It is a condition followed by another waiting and from where I will make my escape.

When I first met Aban he had many questions, imagine my surprise when the answers rolled off my tongue. Then he waited for an interpretation which I also supplied. Such was our giving and taking. I told him in detail how Texas got things done, then I changed the story and told him again. I am open to all manner of explanation provided nothing remains of the telling. It doesn't matter who said what or the village they come from. Here there is only the disappearance of places and things, and on the whole, far too much thinking. The universe won't fit in this room so I keep it inside my head. I drag random pieces laughing and screaming onto an incredulous page. This marks the beginning of my sedentary work, but I do miss the travelling. Hakim says it's a welcome change from my previous service. Together we extol the virtues of my new, ordinary life, but I'm not listening.

The conquistadors were appalled by ritual murder, a blade to the heart. They preferred burning the natives alive and the English strapped them to the mouths of cannons. At every feast, since the beginning of time, there was wine and the killing of animals that were not very fast. Saddam Hussein had his name stamped on each and every brick used to build monuments. As he climbed the scaffold he winked at the President. We'll do this again, he said, several times per millennium. It matters who we are when we die. As for me, I speak everything as if for the second time so I can ask myself what it means. This is called a poetic state. What was once difficult is easier now, but I'm still tortured by how funny things are. That's why I keep a list of all that has happened. I don't want to be astonished by what happens next.

Tomorrow I will set out on foot from my prison cell, inspect where I'm going. I asked Hakim if he would accompany me to examine my future residence. I must go soon, I explained, because later I will be blind. Hakim wasn't listening so I kept on talking. I didn't want him to think I'd run out of options. I didn't want him to see what I already knew, that my eyes were three times their size. Lately I just can't seem to hide my surprise. Hakim mumbled something about a reunion with loved ones and an old man in the sky. That's when I knew he was crazy. Still, I said, I could listen to what the old man had to say. Give him another chance but he shouldn't feel compelled to make an appearance. I like him, but I like him much better when he's not around.

12

In the Holy Land change comes suddenly or not at all. In Gaza it's generally just before breakfast, while the family is showering. The sound of a whistle behind an Israeli cannon and then, no ordinary bustle. A soldier asks for your papers, terrified all that goes through your head is that you don't have your hair on. Your husband is flat on the bathroom floor, still in his underwear. The school bus will be here any minute and he hasn't made the lunches. The children shriek and move to Nunavut to live on icebergs with the walruses. They've left a note. We won't need our voices any more, we've left them on the kitchen table, please ship them to Australia. What's a walrus, your husband wants to know from beneath a soldier's boot, and where the hell is Nunavut.

Deep in a cabinet I found *A Photographic History of Kashmir*, 1934. A remnant from when English boys still dreamt of faraway adventure. The people they conquered, spellbound by the blood and pageantry, would later imitate their enthusiasm. In between the pages was the thin diary of a young mother and two photographs. Her initial entries were a record of first events, first steps, first words. Her father sold vegetables in the market, our good fortune she wrote. In the first picture her grandfather struck a shy pose next to an olive tree, behind the tree this house where I am held prisoner. In the second image his family was all around him, his arms wrapped about the shoulders of a wiry teenage girl. A heap of rusting steel now commemorates where they stood, the olive tree and the young girl, now a mother according to her diary, are missing.

In New York I built a house to contain my trepidation. After I die I will go back there to decipher my last sigh. I am enthralled by the diary of this young woman since it might be the last thing that I read. I can't wait to pick it up again, as soon as I finish my own story. When my son left home

I switched to a better brand of soap and moved to London. Here, I thought, in Shakespeare's alphabet nothing is ever lost or forgotten, and after the industrial revolution the Queen needs much less defending. Still, its bards remain vigilant, secret handshakes and resumés at the ready. Monarchs, if we're to believe the versifiers, die by poison and kill by proxy, there is no record of the victims. Less is more.

In her last entry the girl was writing cards to friends and listening to songs on the radio. Then the helicopters began raining bullets. We ran from room to room, father was at work, God protect him. The furniture was already in the windows. The helicopters left at midnight and then the shelling started. The explosions were much louder than the radio. Across the street a neighbour was hanging, scaling, hand over hand, the edge of his roof. The house was burning and he was trying to get to his daughter's room. It made me shiver, she wrote, and then I was on the floor. I lost all feeling, felt as though I had no legs. I was hoping that I had not been wounded. Finally I realized that it was fear – just fear.

The people of the world are the same and the other. The other is who we want to kill. The bond with our victim cannot be diminished, it cannot be reduced. It is prior to knowledge, sometimes it sounds like prayer. It is a good idea to kill your enemy, just aim for your neighbour. It gets easier. The order eventually comes in the voice of him who obeys it, this is how armies kill each other. That's so the rest of us don't have to do it. We support our troops with an ever-decreasing vocabulary. In a few thousand years they will confirm who was here and who was not. An army of archaeologists is scouring the Israeli landscape. They excavate, catalogue and fix the evidence. They who find the most bones get to live in Jerusalem.

On the Russian steppes greatcoats and blood-soaked rags for your feet were all the rage. A generation in the snow as far as the eye could see, unless you were lucky enough to be among the trees. They waited for vodka which came on trains with men and ammunition. The new arrivals marvelled at the range of German artillery. They were posted to the spaces left behind by the dead, who simply waited. Nothing of what is to come arrives until it is already gone. Fathers disappeared into the Pliocene and countries into maps. Moscow is in Texas finally. In New York we were deciding the twentieth century; a man on the moon with a radio, banker's boxes and Nietzsche, the pocket edition.

The days go on and on and still no sign of my hooded friend. I wait in this room, or is it Nantucket, footsteps on the boardwalk and then a voice. You've been living in the wrong infinity, he says. Hakim is constantly interrupting, he seems to know when I'm rehearsing for a proper ending. He enters with my food, he wants another story. As I speak he imitates my inflection and asks its meaning. He doesn't know that this will hurt him. I ask him when I will die. Soon, he says. He prefers the idiom of the British prisoners. In 1828, I begin, Andrew Jackson extended the right to vote to men without property. More hands were needed to build the gilded age, more signatures for God's army. The pulpit and the law is our tradition. Texas is nothing if not sane, the language plain, you will go mad or join the congregation.

Hakim leaves and the mouse enters: did he say anything about me … no … what about the bird did he talk about the bird … no … the bird can't be trusted … why not … I'll explain later … ok … I got to go to work … what do you do … security … for whom … that's confidential … I see … it's a dangerous world out there … that's true … and it's raining money … I've heard, but you're a mouse … your point … I don't know … it's a great war isn't it … I'm not sure … we needed it … why … the President's approval ratings were dropping … I see … the whole world is our frontier … is it … it's bigger than both of us … I thought so … keep me in the loop will you … what loop … you're in the eye of the storm … I'm in prison … this is the war room … really.

Yesterday I lived in a hut by a lake in some mountain village, Pakistan or Afghanistan, a landscape I invented. Thomas Aquinas lived next door, higher and a little closer to the moon. What do believers want, I asked, knowing he'd written extensively on the matter. Perhaps in my madness I misheard him. Want is what believers do, he said, it wells up in our mouths like vomit. I should have come to these mountains sooner, everything I wrote is straw. From these heights, I explained, entire patrols will one day disappear in the crosshairs of a single gunner. What should I do, he asked. I suggest you start again but this time write the last thing first and listen for the words you'll never hear ... anything else ... if you start to feel weak, kill just one thing and eat it.

This fracture, this hole, as any fish will tell you, is neither round nor square, it's just the shape I'm in. There is so much to do. In the morning I sally forth, forward is a figment of my return. I tell my story to anyone who'll listen, an admiral or the Queen as they sail by on some passing liner. They wait as I pose the same old question, but they won't let me board. Your clothes have turned to rags, they say, and when you're around things only worsen. Their refusal is difficult to hear, especially on such a brilliant day inside my empty room. I miss New York, I scream, and I miss London too ... everything is as you remember it, they assure me, and the rest is hearsay.

I was standing in St. Peter's Square when the Pope gave his last address. Outside the stones were well-trodden, inside, slabs, layers upon layers of imposing corpses. There are no tambourines here and nobody speaks in tongues. The years are flying by, the Pope said, but I have been spared the misfortune of knowing. I'm just a middleman. In Texas, God is the fixed point, the third man and a Republican. The churches don't have balconies but everybody still waves. Percentages are agreed to in advance and absolution is granted after the cheque clears. Researchers examine algorithms and God speaks to the congregation through ten-thousand-watt speakers. After the service everyone goes for breakfast at McDonald's.

The wind whistles through the trees and through my window. I listen and walk to where I am waiting. I do not arrive. This is a murmur in all directions but it is not at a crossroads, there is no choice to make. At night the ocean is a thin black line, in the sun it is beyond our grasp. I am looking for a rumour, a few notes at the end of the world. I will die of boredom or of terror, in either case I'll lose my grip. I know where this ship is going. I reviewed the manifest, checked my ticket and to be sure I read the label on my underwear. When I was with Aban I asked him why his people keep on disappearing. He said it's because we keep on killing them. I've learned a thing or two about navigation. An ocean is impossible to look at and there is no ground beneath my feet.

13

As a diplomat I wore a white suit, buttons and bones. I carried my head in a canvas sack. I made all of my appointments before the end, more or less in the middle. I heard the first word and the last, nothing in between. I modified towns, ash and scrap iron. I starved the living and buried the dead with a bulldozer. I was the future. In New York I woke at six in the morning to run along the river. There was plenty of heavy equipment there too, but it was used to backfill foundations, gas and water mains. In the mornings I used a crowbar to pry my face from the pillow. It was like a frying pan so I splashed it with a little water. Slapped and punched it until it resembled my point of view.

As children in Calabria we killed lizards with arrows fashioned from the spokes of weapons-grade umbrellas. Only the English still make umbrellas like that. We buried them on a hill, each with a crucifix of sticks and string. The biggest one was smaller than your baby sister, but when you bury a lizard no one gets in line to shake your hand. The nuns kept the young women of our town busy with the apocalypse and embroidery. Moths all over Europe celebrated the tradition. There was no food to match the fine table linen so we played through lunch, and then we played through dinner. The needlework would be preserved for the next generation, a hope chest for your sister unless your cousin Maria was prettier.

After Aban's friends brought our lunch into the courtyard they chased the children into the bowels of broken buildings. There, the little ones could avoid the heat and dream in the cooling shadows that one day it would be their turn to eat. A town sleeps, but high above the clouds the sun never sets. It is neither night nor day. It is time. Previously a pilot had to ask a foot soldier, perhaps over a couple of beers, as to the efficacy of his work. His instruments could only find the edge of things and from such altitudes targets have a way of drifting, a way of dodging their insignificance. These days everywhere there are budding filmmakers, and there's no better content than a massacre. The victims will never know their notoriety. We have nothing against the Palestinians, they just can't live here.

Before my capture the President dispatched the Vice President to the war. His name was Dick. Dick speaks for the President or the other way around. The palace was frantic, everything had to be named and fit inside his mouth in the form of an answer, a question or a stick. He took a suite on a middle floor, facing north. He too wanted to stay cool. He gave the army a list of Texas staff and made-over locals. Bathrooms were assigned and we were rounded up and brought to the castle. Aban was on Dick's list. The Vice President wants to see me … apparently … he is a wise and powerful man ... some would disagree ... when will he receive us … they'll let us know … I will prepare my report ... what report.

Aban was searched at the castle entrance and again during breakfast. The Vice President sits next to the President, he explained. In the waiting room he reviewed his notes like a field mouse at the gate. First find out what he wants, I suggested. Yes of course. On entry an orderly was serving tea, the garrison was perfectly still. Aban walked and talked. Mr. Vice President I have seen your trucks … what trucks … Halliburton … they're not my trucks … I understand. Sir, together we will put a chicken and a radish on every table. All distribution points are on existing routes. Texas pays for the trucks empty or full. Economists are predicting slow and fast growth in China, plenty of work and plenty of hunger. After the war we will still need chickens, and I'll show you what you can do with a radish.

I am not ready to live in a world without grammar. I'm safe here so long as I stay with the thought that approaches. It's not mine exactly because I can't see myself in it. It's just a statement that changes. I wish, instead, I had a field to plant or a violin, snug as a knife beneath my chin to keep me from the very next word. I don't want to be the future anymore, some half-baked integer lodged in the repeating zero of a clock, a fingerprint looking for a body. If you can hear me Lord call in an air strike, and try not to hit this building. When I am saved I will work every harvest until my arms ache and my hands blister. I will only talk to heads made of wheat between ears of corn, and then only with a click of my tongue.

God loves the wealthy. For Aristotle too democracy was tolerable if it were limited to the few. The wretched covet their neighbours' goods, he observed. The rich must be spared. Two thousand years later James Madison, swimming and drowning in ink, put it in the constitution. Now we are the wealth of nations and God protects us from the poor. For the indigent and the dispossessed, Madison explained, food will be too expensive. Religion is the key and after that door opens, we'll slam it. I discussed the matter with Hakim but I didn't want us to get confused, so I did all the talking. The bird was there, being dead he contributed nothing to the conversation, but he could have.

In Texas what we don't know is a pre-existing condition. God, it seems, sometime after the seventh day managed to switch the conversation. From now on death matters, he said, and suddenly we all had a future. There were soldiers with helmets and little pieces of lead we could catch with our chest. Boys basking in a posthumous kiss at the end of every era. In Vietnam they became men, or hightailed it to Canada. After every war comes redemption, but your sweetheart will have moved on. But that doesn't make you any less of a hero. Two dead in a bed, and then the killer made himself a sandwich. In Texas we take care of our own and sometimes we do it on television. A cheeseburger, fries and a Pepsi, a slow walk with a few friends who still wear the uniform, then face up on a slab. This, of course, is just an example, some prefer steak. Death in plus or minus five minutes.

The people of this desert have told us all they know. The few who refused are spitting up blood in undisclosed prisons. This place is buttoned down tighter than a Mississippi warehouse with dogs and a brand new computer. Though for reasons we don't understand, people in vests are spontaneously exploding.

Hakim said that's how you fight a war without airplanes. As for stragglers, the bodies we left in the rubble – you wouldn't believe the numbers – Rumsfeld is doing his best to make them go away. There's the army and then there's the army that makes the facts. It's from them that we get our instructions. It's not a plan exactly. This week we're interrogating seagulls.

Dear Dick: I've done what I could and for the most part our targets have been immobilized, but I regret to report that I've been captured. Everyone says we missed the point but I am sure that one day school children will be paraded past a carving of your severed head. Don't worry about the long view, it belongs to the pigeons. Tell us, for example, how you planned the war and then waited for the reason, finally wrenched from the citadels where money is thought. The best and the brightest jumping out of windows, it just doesn't get any better than this. Your own presence in retreat, everybody liked George more anyway. Is that when you decided there would be no coffins in the official record? This is the truth about solitude, Dick, when it ceases to be musing it is madness itself, and we never escape prosecution.

The bird you dispatched arrived last week, or yesterday. He has unleashed a tidal wave of democracy and the mouse too seems to have his eye on the prize but I can't confirm anything either of them are saying. Apparently the bird cannot disclose my location but he has promised to deliver this note. I have no choice but to believe him. My cell is comfortable enough, never humid and finally I've had time to think. I wish to be done with the desert, its slumber and its heat. Peace is the making of a threat, it is armed to the teeth. War is the same welcome, the same rupture. I am your host and hostage, your friend and prisoner. I will kill you at the end of my goodness. I will bludgeon you with a peace process.

14

I HAVE PUT ALL the animals on notice. After an air raid, dead cats next to dead people may befuddle a goat but goats don't have the words to express their confusion. Still there's no reason for concern, nestled as we are behind the perfect yarn. We are on the right side of history. In Jerusalem Yahweh keeps busy peopling the air. In Idaho a mother lets one tear drop for no one but herself. For several thousand years we have been waging our disputes. Between one war and the next we catch up on our sleep, rebuild houses to better trap the sun. I am trying to find the thread in these old tales, allow me to explain. God does not exist and he has abandoned you. Between nothing and almost nothing there is the moon's bald head, and settlements that multiply like boots upon your neck.

Nine eleven gave us nine eleven and some other numbers of which this is not a complete list. We cannot count the dead in the same way everywhere. I have noticed there is a bias against the carnage winning brings. The media will improve the situation, put only our dead on every channel. We decide, supply and train the enemy, we are the keepers of accredited space and events, the guardians of who will speak. Everyone is disappearing slowly, this is how Texas builds its inventory. Let us accept this hypothesis and proceed patiently. Who will speak for the New York dead, of sadness without end on the small screen? There is no need to recall Hiroshima and, it's in the wrong hemisphere. The truth of salvation endures inside the profane.

In the thirties we huddled round the radio, we got our vegetables from a moving truck. Tap was all the rage on those cold Chicago nights. Bojangles and Shirley Temple, heel to toe in the best establishments. If you couldn't afford a ticket your teeth could stand in for the stars, unless you walked the streets half lit or had long johns on underneath your trousers. Those who had money did not speak of it and Jesus never mixed up the marching orders, or the guest list to the mayoral prayer breakfast. Place mattered. He showed us how to manage the utensils, a few tricks with a knife then swallow. Ants live below the grass and are the sum of what they carry. Remember to bend your knees and put your back into it. If you're black learn to tap.

In New York everything was close by because I had no place to go. I worked a window in the sky and took an interest in the things that did not interest me. I watched the glass bend the branches on which the squirrel delighted in the senseless joy of its not falling. I do not know what it was thinking, sound and gesture, the truth before, a clatter inside the presumption of its birth. I know this reasoning is rife with rumour and what's worse, poor alliteration. But I am surviving my oblivion, year after year and always the same day. What I don't know is worth mentioning, but the details aren't worth the energy. Only a caterpillar will hang up its carcass and move on to better things, worldly in a new suit of clothes.

I have seen what I have not seen. The imprint at large of skyscrapers in quick collapse in the real time of say, Moose Factory, Ontario, an independent and properly constituted jurisdiction with at least one rumour of poetry, and now herald to a tale of living weapons to the south. A symphony on the evening news, a dream-guided cluster of elegance and focused in the old style. A legend of two towers next to a river the day we perished. Soon it will have happened long ago. The brave people of New York have awakened the President to repeated and random announcements of unspecified terror from the east. Between Europe and Asia approximately, and agreeing, more or less, on a few countries just north of Africa.

The mouse is back and he wants to know if Texas has sent representation … they sent a bird, a dead bird … anyone else … I'm not sure … the bird is just trying to make a name for himself … I don't think he has a name … tell him to fly back to New York … he doesn't listen to me … I see … how's the war going … the army is retreating … did we lose … I don't think so … that's good … have the Texas messengers come … who … the Texas messengers, couriers, attachés, representatives, two of them … I'm not sure … you met them in New York … oh yes, those guys … well … well what … have they come … I'm not sure … how can you not know … lately there's been a lot of coming and going … they would be hard to miss … why two … would you prefer one, or three … I don't understand … they report to the President … I see … well … well what … pick a number … two is fine … let me know when they get here.

The President is a good old boy and a champion of ordinance striking at the imagination. Silhouettes on the horizon, Tom Cruise and – that other guy. You might say we approach from the inside, the hollow expansion of image and rumour, armed and virtual without a name and where we are not seen. It is the absence of language that interests us. The line that lends itself to our appropriation and any means necessary. A simple matter of apparatus in place angled to never quite correspond. In anonymity find direction, heavenward some would say, since it swallows the dead and the living. It becomes us. From the Manchurian Mountains to the Polish border, it is best, we suggest, if you sleep fully dressed.

I'm talking here, and moving toward an aspect of the same, chronology all at once and the promise that Texas delivers. We are practiced in the rule of killing and letting die. Geography is merely the medium through which the arrangement of technology is transmitted and necessary for locating an open threat. Words belong to the spaces in between, the violence to come which we must disarm with bombs that are never smart enough. Japan is abuzz with greed and fashion. A new generation of noses, row on row pressed against fenestration, portholes to what they're wearing in New York or L.A., the Manhattan Project finally come to fruition. The weapon that is not here yet is forever.

At the beginning of this century Tommy Franks took to the skies to deliver freedom's burden. On longer trips he took his wife. His seat had four stars next to her four hearts. They were married in Oklahoma where wives get lost in the dustbowl if you don't chain them to something, the sofa or a lamppost. Tommy felt good in the atmosphere. He had no quarrel with death, its surplus or its unclenched fist. Bombs fall below the clouds, lodge in a cupful of dirt or an ear. The software Texas uses to forecast civilian casualties is called bug-splat. One morning Rumsfeld decided only the President could be Commander-in-Chief, Franks would be just a commander. Tommy liked to watch movies with his wife on long flights. His favourite was *The Nutty Professor* and he didn't give a rat's ass what Rumsfeld called him.

Butterflies are not birds and only airplanes have radios. If a bird flies into a building it loses its shape but no one pays much attention because it is so small and there are no people on it. All over the world people squint because they can't believe what they're seeing. When a plane collides with a New York tower the dust settles in Kandahar. But it doesn't matter, seeing as there are more recruits than corpses. A shoulder and a steady hand is all you need to fire an RPG. In these hills a gunner will do more to end the war than all the talking heads in Washington. If his hands could speak they'd be pointless. Words insinuate, that's why knowing is not in this or any other sentence, along with the peace that was never mentioned.

Before I was captured I told Aban that one day we would forget this war. You have to be alive to forget, he said. Saddam Hussein used to be our son of a bitch and then we changed our minds. After which he slept in a different house every night and never talked on the telephone. Before Texas came to liberate his people with one hundred and seventy-five thousand troops, tanks and a lot of airplanes he told his snipers to climb palm trees to get a better shot at the enemy. He, like Tommy Franks, knew the war would be won in the skies. Evil, Tommy explained to his wife over a few margaritas, is consecutive, the red man, the rebel south and the red menace followed by Osama Bin Laden. Then they drank to their own good fortune.

15

In Calabria we gathered mushrooms and hunted hare but we ate more pigs because we could outrun them. We knew what there was to know about the weather. Our days were mostly echoes and smells. Gypsies foretold our death for a morsel and promised the hills would still whisper our name. You had to walk through the clouds to get to our town. We boasted more songs than cars in a dialect no one else could understand, and we were suspicious of all other languages. I knew nothing of the suffering below. Eventually Texas showed me how to match my wardrobe to the conversation, how to mimic the first person singular. When they knocked on my door I was ready to work.

I paid my rent in advance and sailed an iceberg to the Sudan. My instructions were to secure the carbon sequence, crystals to die for. They were disappearing in their raw immensity into the body cavities of the workers who mined them. I needed to put an end to their insolence, be it by confession or spectacle. I needed to set an example. I fired everyone who was spitting up blood and I told the shift supervisors to report those racked with fever. Then I addressed the remainder. Dear brothers and sisters, it is late and so I'll be brief, your salvation is in the things you can't keep. Nowhere in your wretched lives will you have occasion to wear diamonds, and trading them for rice is blasphemy on Park Avenue.

We have become disarticulated in these modern times, brains will no longer be swept off the floor. Apparently there's not enough money to clean up the mess, where's the protocol to climb back from the ruins. The truth belongs to us, of course, the long and the shorter view. In the late morning sky a rocket no bigger than a pencil stops, thinks for a moment and changes its direction. A woman and a cat, still in their pyjamas, follow it from the window. They're a little depressed so they forgot to get dressed. They watch as the missile strikes the market where they would routinely be shopping and drinking tea. As for the people already there, it's too late to save them. There's no point going out anymore, said the woman as she crawled back into bed. I agree, said the cat.

Mr. President, Saddam invited us in and we combed every inch of this place, scoured every cave and factory. Explain to me again why we could not take yes for an answer. A picture is what we say it is but it's hard to catalogue things that aren't there, and the bunkers were empty before we went in. Still there is much to learn from the knickknacks that get left behind, cold tea, stale bread on the kitchen table, homework on the living room floor. People don't die when they should, they're always in the middle of something, waiting for us to leave, for example. Home is home, tangled up in a railway track or under a heap of concrete. Home is home even after the heart stops beating. These people will never abandon their dead. Mr. President, the Third Reich is buried in Dachau, not the other way around, there where flowers now grow.

Closure is a policy of encirclement adopted in 1993 to lay siege to Gaza and The West Bank. A wall in the middle of a field will generally disturb a farmer's routine, disrupt cities. These are things best seen on your feet, and the walk to Jordan or Egypt will do you good. Keep moving. In Israel they are hearing voices first heard at the beginning of the world. It's a story about messengers in loose linen with trumpets, and women with flowers reporting on prophets and kings. Always the hope of a hope elsewhere, followed by a fall, the last bit of light before towers fall. Then, like now, the world was full of patriotic asses. I told Hakim that I'm writing a book about it. The executioner must wait, and then I will write an addendum.

Someone once told me of a poem so big that it had to be carried by an elephant. It was years in preparation, perhaps decades. The poet had no interest in the work and so described everything perfectly. On his deathbed he began to speak calmly, of planets and faces, slowly, of every birch tree, but to whom I don't know. I think he was on the side of the living. On the very last day and for the sake of the archive he numbered the pages. Now it rots in eternity. This will explain everything, he said, though I never once wrote what I thought. I didn't want to make things worse. The poet entrusted me with the translation, from Russian to Greek or the other way around. I speak neither and so I took my cue from a kangaroo.

The bird is back and he too is asking about the Texas messengers. The mouse said they report to the President, I explained ... the mouse is an ass, they report to me ... then why are you asking me ... everything has to go through your head ... I see, will they bring confirmation ... who ... the Texas messengers ... no ... clarification ... no ... instructions ... no ... a hint ... no ... a wink ... it's not clarity that matters ... oh ... it's the coming and going ... I see ... first one then the other ... have you been back to Texas ... I'm stationed in Berlin ... that's a lot of flying ... flying doesn't bother me just the headache I get from hitting things ... oh ... but I don't mind getting a headache once in a while ... I see ... being dead, I am also blind ... how do you decide on a direction ... I decide where I'm going after I get there ... I don't understand ... Berlin is where I say it is.

Before Harvard I lived in Chicago, wind-scorched skyscrapers on Lake Michigan. In the winter I listened to the blues and rolled my own cigarettes. There was a woman, olive gold in a white dress. When I met her she was beating the bushes for her next meal. I put a credit card between her thighs to protect her from that frozen city. She burned through the limit faster than a stock tip at a Texas barbecue. When the light finally fell from her eyes I asked what went wrong. You have all that I want in this wind and this snow, she said, but this city never retires a debt. Marry me, I said. No, it is better to lose than to win as you do. My grandfather, she said, was brought to these shores but he never agreed. He talked to his horn and slept on his fist. He cut his meat with a pocket knife.

I don't know what time it is and Hakim is only reporting his next visit. In Egypt stones keep the record but I do not think they will remember me. The last several decades have been good for everybody except the maimed and the dead. I am discussing strategy with a bird and economics with a mouse. I wake, wash myself and already it is night. There is no time. The words from this room have abandoned me and are looking for what death will uncover, a flower broken or missing, a forkful of nothing. I have only this flimflam, what I have imagined of barbed wire and fingers unbuttoning a blouse. There on display, next to the alley where slaves sing and dance, is where I put things that are, and things that have never been.

I used to read the old poets and then a beast licked my ear. Now I am waiting to come back from an errand, some place I've never been. I hope it's Australia and then I will tell myself what I saw. I hear there are slums near the harbour but never enough liquor to kill your own stench. I want to be in Chicago again, afraid with a woman's breast in each hand. Or turn this thing around in Luxembourg, where there is so much money the enemy, they say, never stops loving you. I want to go back to the courtyard with Aban before the light was removed from his eyes. I want to withdraw my name from death row, throw my voice into a glacier and wait for it on the other side.

I am the accused. I did what I did and now I'm looking for the day after. It never arrives. Yesterday I was happy. Pictures with Santa Claus, youth badges and trophies, the letter I wrote to the President. Worlds come and go. I keep the dead near. What is near is not familiar at all. The people here say it is we who are strange. They do not understand why we've come. Did the army take a wrong turn, did a supply clerk write down the wrong address? How stupid is the state to defend against weapons that do not exist? Praise be the King, he does not love us but he is well versed in the hereafter, or we'll soon find out. A missile, he says, is smarter than Einstein and not at all abstract when explaining what's what to an atom.

I sleep a lot these days, as if in molten tin. I am awakened in the night by the Texas messengers, they are asking for my report. When this war is over, I begin, we will need to rethink, retool and retrain … go on … elect a President who cannot decide, hire teachers who do not know and appoint judges who are not sure … what else … we need ships that sink, planes that fall and bombs that miss … are you done … we will honour the soldier who just can't go on and the general who swallows his gun … go to the end … we will remain still, knee deep in the people we killed … this is not the report we were looking for … I'm sorry … we need you to write a rebuttal … shouldn't somebody else do that … just change your mind, then … come back in an hour.

16

In 1945 we split the atom and became a world power. Death is ordinary in that it happens to everyone. In Japan it was just one scene, from the inside of a snow globe. The sky flipped to its opposite and saw its own likeness, the same hollow without the oxygen. Butterflies and dragonflies, frogs with their loose necks must have died first. People stopped for an instant and then the dialogue took wing. "I've never seen anything like this before." Curtain falls. Afterwards there were droughts and the demand for British umbrellas took a turn for the worse. Nothing grew, and rounding up a duck was the highlight of the month and every meal for a week. People darned socks and patched the holes in their pants. Fashion, it seems, had abandoned the Japanese.

In 1947 I was in Washington working on the Truman Doctrine. My job was to write the sentence and its negation, who had who, and who had who with an axe. History happens twice, the President explained, and then he told us about his Containment Policy. Its purpose was to contain everything long enough for us to take it. Almighty God intends us to lead, Truman said. The first order of business was to help the fascists in Greece defeat the mountain partisans who had fought against Hitler. We didn't need them anymore, that's how we knew they were communists. The French were rebuilding their country and Parisians were leaving New York. They said we had no style and no sense.

Every morning Hakim brings me coffee, it helps me to work. He says today is the first day of autumn. At the first opportunity I'll drive to up-state New York to confirm it. The leaves will tell me what I need to know. This room is worse than the dream I woke up from. I can't sit still, the coffee is strong and panic hunts for each waking cell. I stand at the kitchen counter or pace until the words come to me. I cancel a few each day and then I bury the premise. What is said must be unsaid, what is unsaid is reasonable and bears repeating. To be clear, the previous two sentences don't say anything. Death too, is a really good trick, so my Grandfather said in a note. At least so far, he wrote, it's my most successful idea. It must be true because he never sent another.

After the war everyone was looking for a better life so we invented Tupperware, turkey and all the trimmings, sandwiches long after Thanksgiving. All the Russians in Manhattan changed their name to Rick. Toward the end of the decade the President phoned me, he gave me a briefcase full of contracts and threats to take to Japan. Before my departure I called him. Perhaps we should give this a little more thought, I suggested. We've administered the enema, he said, now go and collect the bill. I took a wrong turn at Kashmir and ended up in China. Soon we were importing fine silk and Asians. The women in Manhattan no longer had to do their own sewing.

By 1959 we had put the Second World War on display for the next generation to see on their way to Vietnam. In Texas junkyards were filled to capacity, in Mexico everybody was looking for used parts. British men were mourning the loss of the empire and putting the touch on the missus. Honey, give us a kiss and a bob for a pint. In Frankfurt, on Tuesdays I think, they were rationing meat without flies. The Nazis were fine but for the genocide. What ties us to each other is a dry box of matches, the body count from the next town. In 1942 they gave us this house, fully furnished, but no one could explain the unmade beds and dirty dishes. It was situated next to a bombed out concert hall. For a decade or so no one had to sit through a sonata, and then they rebuilt it.

When the bank pulls the trigger on that dollar you borrowed, the same dollar they lent your neighbour and so on down the block, they won't ask any questions because they'll already have the answers. That's what the founding fathers intended and before they drafted the Constitution they agreed that an agreement is not an agreement, and then they agreed not to tell anyone else. This, and smallpox, is how we outlasted the red man. What the founding fathers knew is that stone walls are not thick enough. The next time the people storm the Bastille the king won't be there. He's the tiger in your tank, he's on the shelf at your local superstore, next to the mayonnaise. He's the sun in Peru.

Mobility is a fundamental right of the substantial people and money is always looking for new places to go. Washington just sold its debt to the English, twice, and then they sold it again to the Chinese. Adam was naked out of the gate so I put him in a car and we drove nonstop to Milan. He never looked back. So this is the real world, he said, and what they call chic, so much to gather, so much to keep. That's when we knew he was one of us. Soon he was writing books on all aspects of government, theology and business. Everyone he endorsed rose in the polls. Nothing begets a lot in Tibet, he explained, but in Tennessee it lodges itself in a petrified skull. In Tennessee the people need something to do.

Adam and his wife are retired now and living in Arizona though he still works behind the scenes and together they throw the best dinner parties. They never tired of apples. In 1943 Adam began to dismantle Roosevelt's New Deal. It's an ontological distinction, he explained, we're giving the country back to the angels. When Reagan was elected he breathed a sigh of relief. Poverty, he told the President, is the clear result of spiritual transgression and legislation must be aligned with the divine. What is God like, I asked, while sitting on Adam's back porch with a warm cognac and a cigar, the lights glistening all the way to the Mexican border. He's not a flexible man, he said, I guess that's why his son had to die.

After Japan buried their crumpled dead the people remained loyal and ready to rise but they were hoping the order wouldn't come. The country, for the most part, remained populous but they were no longer reporting deaths on the evening news and birds that remained had to content themselves with fewer trees. Government offices stayed lit through the night, everything needed updating. People rolled up their sleeves and began deleting names for the next census. Scientists too researched till dawn and then reported back to the Emperor. Their primary concern was the sperm count. The Emperor immediately signed the surrender on the *USS Missouri* and then MacArthur told him to get out of Korea. Korea had not yet come to its senses, it was not ready for independence. It was in desperate need of a containment policy.

Ask your doctor if this is right for you.

The public relations business cleans up our wars and runs our elections when they're not selling shampoo. In 1950 McCarthy showed up with a list, it made things a lot easier. Finally we knew right from wrong, but disagreement was possible if you didn't need your job. On Sunday we sang every word, the pastor said the songs would protect us from the people who rent. In 1952 we elected Eisenhower, a no-nonsense God-fearing man. We gave our lives to him and to Procter and Gamble. It was our world to end. God was opening subdivisions in the best constellation, on every star a new putting green. The Russians could have Nantucket after we'd gone. But it's not over, McCarthy cautioned, there are still the Arabs and the Chinese and nobody knows anything about the Norwegians.

Texas abstained from a Security Council resolution to prosecute the genocide in Darfur. Then they prevented the United Nations from funding the investigation. Everywhere thought accumulates, but in Amarillo they are as dumb as concrete. Texas, we are at your service, in step and available on demand. We are living in your sitcoms, waiting with bated breath in the pews of Oklahoma. We are keeping you safe in our mouths. We are exchanging recipes and tips on cholesterol. We are making small breasts bigger and big breasts smaller. We are trying to lose weight in record numbers. But we forgot the name of that dictator we cannot ignore.

When my wife and I lived in New York we never chased autographs. We told everyone that linoleum was making a comeback and we always hit the mark between whimsy and horror. We practiced practicing and learned how to hang a word on a pause. We read poets who did not burn in the atmosphere but knew it was there. Our friends were of the opinion that not everyone had to be somebody's wife. We were in Rome in sixty-eight but for the life of us we could never remember the century. The architecture refused to give up its secrets but still we were admired for the choices we made. On Park Avenue we know what the killing is for.

The mouse said that I will not be around for old age, that muddle from which we do not return. What should I do, mouse ... what do you mean, do ... my life is not where I put it ... have you looked under the bed ... yes ... really ... who will I be when I am missing ... you're missing now ... oh ... that's why everybody is looking for you ... what about after I'm dead ... you'll still be missing ... I see ... you will be what is in you of the other ... so I'll be remembered ... don't exaggerate ... I don't understand ... this is not about you ... what a situation ... try to make the best of it ... how ... find something bigger than yourself ... God ... a Boeing on its way to New Jersey.

17

In Texas what we need is what we get, but we no longer have to put it on layaway. Everything goes on the credit card for which we need not apply because they already have our information. Things are delivered directly to our brain so there's always room for something else. When the head is full there's the garage and then straight to the landfill. Check the card's expiration date and don't worry about the rate, it's buried on page forty-eight. For every transgression there's a new dotted line but we would be remiss if we didn't suggest quarters more suitable to your situation. Please don't take this personally, you are this and not some other person, it would take forever to get that corrected. Who is who or the other way around, and who made the future come earlier.

When I first came to this desert I still loved the President, but what we were up to, you don't want to know. There were nights when we stopped the mercury from falling. If I ever get out of here I will describe things much better but I have no intention of making myself understood. Not I, but a slippery who, will squander what remains of the language, terror's meddling half note. Then I will swallow my tongue. Hakim said I should have a plan to prepare for what happens next. I told him that I will save the last day for my executioner, dance with the one that brung me. Until then I'll do what I do best, work the room. I'm the life of the party with a pocket full of phone numbers, but I wish to say bluntly, one last time, it's not me on the line.

Hakim said today is a holiday … what's the occasion … God … yours or mine … there is only one … yes of course. At midday, approximately, I found wisdom. I hope it doesn't happen again. Now I am smaller than a fly and bigger than all human invention. Planets only last an hour and everything dies before it takes to the sky. Finally there can be no dispute, a moment is longer than the future. Night after night I walk these stones, barefoot from the window to the door, and then to the Mexican border. Hakim says the fever is normal and what happens below is subtracted above. He always says what he means. I have all that I need in this room, a body temperature, a pail and a window, without which the sun and the moon would cease to exist.

On March 3, 2002 Tommy Franks and I met with the President to express our concern with the lack of membership in the new coalition. On or about the same time Saddam Hussein was explaining to his generals that they must have won the last war or they would not be meeting. That's a fact. I was back and forth with the weapons inspectors, showing them how to take pictures of things that do not exist, and how to think, so that they would not think otherwise. Sometimes we met in France, cozy evenings in cafés. Its philosophers, after the monarchy, were the masters of indecision, ten notches above the Germans, or eight. Everything they did and didn't say is important. For example, a gun or a rope, in Paris I just couldn't decide.

I am looking for the rhythm that a hammer makes, the steady pounding of things felt. I will run aground after my annihilation. I have been given a chance to return to the distance return permits. Death will tell me everything. In my room the bird is tapping his foot on the table, well he said … well what … have they been here … who … the mouse, the messengers, you know who … you do realize this is a locked room, a prison … you're not going to hide behind the facts now are you … I suppose not … well … what is it that you need from them … what I need, this has nothing to do with what I need … oh … there are women half naked on the beach … and … dreams visit me year after year with losses I thought had ended … this is not making sense, bird … it's the only conversation we have … is it necessary … I'll consult with the editor.

The border is where the beginning is received, barred and ended. From Texas we come and go, with pocketfuls of candy. Swallow often to ease the pressure in your eardrums. Children do not die like you and me, on that day they are not caught waiting for the next. They're scaling Everest, a ripped up mattress on a rubbish heap. It's too late to tell their story now, besides, the news would be too big for us. They lie beneath the stones a few steps from their front door, in numbers so the world is still theirs to inherit. They are the milk inside the cactus. I fill my head instead with memories of tiny balconies in Manhattan, afternoon conversations with my neighbour, an actor from Montana always in his underwear.

In this room I think of something and then I write it down. When I yawn it shortens my supposition. I sleep the moment lunch is over. If someone picking up my trail should find an infant dead inside an iceberg, let him be. It's not a sign and he knew the weather would outlast him. Numbers are what they say they are but they're always someone else's. In 2004 there were two thousand, two hundred and twenty-five children in American prisons, a handful in Israel, South Africa and two in Tanzania. The UN Convention on the Rights of the Child was ratified by every member state except the United States and Somalia. I am hoping Texas is looking for someone else to take my place.

With the advent of the industrial revolution death no longer served the king. The captains of industry had need of the puzzled herd, from the age of, say, ten. In Texas we shipped them in from Africa to reduce in-process inventory. In a Security Council resolution of April 2005 we voted against the right to food. A strapping democracy cannot yield to its electorate or its client nations. In better Manhattan the cheese is named and grated at your table. I speak to the bird of those stirring to a fashionable consumption for all things Asian ... what, the buzzing ... no, the drowning. When Texas comes to your town they'll bring all you'll ever need, except a way out.

There are four hundred and four churches in Mobile, Alabama. That's just too many churches and there are even more tin shanties. After the warming comes the ice age and even Shakespeare can't survive that. Beckett might, and a few cockroaches. When the weather breaks again we'll abandon digital and go back to stone. This perhaps is what is meant by the second coming. A bard will grow old while carving a handful of poems. Soon after we'll reinvent the bomb, but I digress, it's the interim that concerns me. Something must be done before the weather changes. This is not it.

The last century was murder and God himself decided the last day. In the beginning the sun rose for me every morning, the Texas wind is slow and from the south. Now I pray, because I don't know how to pray. It's how I keep the heavens underfoot. I move between the window and a busted chair. Hakim recounts everything that I have done and what I have forgotten. When he's not here it all comes in through the keyhole. On days such as this I don't know why death fails to knock. I should have lived differently, he says, or perished sooner. After the war Hakim will leave this place for a land beyond the desert. In Sweden, he says, the corpses don't pile up like garbage.

In the Pacific War I was a ham operator in a mango tree, mangos for breakfast, lunch and dinner. I could see everything except the Japanese. The airflow from the southeast lifted the birds high above my nest. Birds don't give war the attention it deserves and when flying over the harbour they can't tell one ship from another. Life is simpler when you're up a tree. Here, a monkey's feet need never touch the ground and when he dies his friends will not say he's gone elsewhere. Monkeys know there is no better place. After the war I packed my things and climbed down from the tree. Don't leave, the animals said to me, there are still plenty of mangos and surely we have not exhausted every conversation. I'm not going far, I said, look for me in a banana tree in Korea.

A stirring and a wink, a rumour is all I need. Spectators gather round the scaffold, the eternal has begun. The condemned man is the opposite of the king. Things are because they do not belong to him, and that includes the sun and wind. Before he dies he will be quite mad, his body broken, but why this harping on what was? In seventeenth century Spain the accused could not attend his own trial, if he were innocent he would not be in prison. In the seventeenth century Texas was Spanish, and in Guantanamo they're repeating the experiment. It's unfortunate the monarchy had to end. In those days God spoke directly to the king, all campaigns were holy wars not massacres, to help people learn the difference between a pancake and a sphere.

The war to end all wars is still sizzling in the pan, the poet's ghost approaches from afar. His dead are logging their own osteology, mapping the shrapnel all around them. At last, a record we can count on. We know from the caves in France art was invented by a bear, that is its hidden meaning. A few scratches mark the day that we were born. There is enough life in every death, a mother weeps, waiting lengthens, history braces for the anthropologist. Bones don't rest, is the first rule of separation. Darwish begins his song after the world ends and so there is no house for you to sleep in. His poems will be your country now, tears and laughter on a moth's wing.

18

Hakim works his prisoners with a steady smile. He has mastered separation, I'm still translating the translation. In the morning he brings me food and sometimes he complains. Yesterday Texas soldiers played ping-pong with his head. It's a game of waiting for every intermission and then waiting for it to end. I eat, pack a few things and go to the Carolinas, there everyone is getting on just fine without me. No one notices that I have lost my mind but if asked I will explain that I and the universe are loosely stitched. To mask my trepidation I protest the long queues at the liquor store. I leave a note for the waitress at the all-night diner, come save me and try not to drown between the coffee counter and the door. If you hear screaming it's the dreaming. I hate the place I'm in.

I return to my room a faithful dog, a man of letters but nothing is familiar in the words that I bring back. The Carolinas have a certain appeal, war heroes and all my favourite ball players in the wax museum. There, at least, death has a future. I have ruined everything but I'm not finished. If I ever get out of here I will go to Buckingham Palace and ambush the English. I hope it will not take long because next to the Queen's roses you can't pitch a tent. They know all about you and even more about the peoples they've not met. For centuries they had a stake in every calamity, in every sack of flour. We will need them when the world ends again, but this time they should attend. Lately the Queen has been confessing to a few of the empire's minor defects, but in the Sinai they find her sincerity tiresome.

Ready, steady – go, again. Mr. President, I heard of a poet, Russian obviously, who lived in an octopus with a couple of guys who played the ukulele. They served the captain, Nemo I think. In a letter to Blanche he explained his situation at length. The ship he was on capsized but I don't know if he was on his way to Venice or if he was travelling during or in between wars. He said the two musicians were savages and so I am assuming they only performed at weddings and some corporate functions. How they learned to play the ukulele is never made clear. The poet is dead now and no longer reporting his whereabouts. We have only his work and a few letters. Poets need words only while they are alive, we know this because we have yet to receive a message from this or any other dead poet.

In the sixteenth century I sailed with the Puritans to the new world. London was happy to see us go. We were soldiers on Christ's side, victory and our bride adorned – Reagan's kingdom come. Prophecy and genetic drift hath cleared our title to this place. In 1939, West Germany was for the Germans and later Cold War Christians. History is like an old clock with a pendulum except you can't load it onto the back of a pickup truck, or will it to your nephew. As for the victims, there are none, there never were, and they will not be forgiven. God attacks before first light, miracles ablaze in every town and such interesting cuisines. The world is our inheritance, gold and this rod of iron, buckets and buckets of teeth.

In England they do not empty their own spittoons and they keep their elephants in India, the dossier in Piccadilly. The killers on our side are men of peace. Nothing is ever heard of contrition for crimes measured by their absence. I wish I was more like Vallejo, then I could write this with my big toe. We are the king's sons, the clamour of boots and tongues, the story that a story makes. Content and form are of equal importance in the destruction of one then the other, establishing both. Words bend like water through a swamp, very troubling. To speak is to say exactly nothing. Hakim brings me the news and an occasional hardboiled egg. Both are bigger than my head.

I paid down a mortgage or two and then I began to ramble, but I don't believe the things I say, my meagre grief, my full-throated accusations. Hakim showed me the video he took of my arrival. He says I've been all around the world. I look for clues, a New York pretzel or a Texas tan. It is obvious that I'm not in it, alone. Hence the shape I'm in. If you need me, I'll be holed up in the footnotes. A flea knows more than I do but he won't get into print. When this work is over I will lobby to have it banned and then I'll begin again. I was born to save the world or kill a child, doing nothing is the hardest thing. Perhaps this year I will go south for the winter, but I do not mind the cold.

This is neither here nor there, a glimmer of the weed that I was before my mouth took my eyes. Words are tapping on the window, knocking at the door, this room is where they come to get away. In Manhattan they followed me in and out of the shower and to the breakfast table. A child sits dry as wood next to his mother. He is thinking about the rules of multiplication, the eight times table, how it always starts again. Her neck is broken amid ruins that are still smouldering, her face flat against a rock. Now he has one care only, to free himself from this moment. He sees all the colours and her ripped mouth. But it's not true, everyone survived and in his pocket are two tickets to a show. The best perspective, he now realizes, is from the inside of a tank or an apartment in Manhattan. On the lease is some guy named Dave. Eight times one is eight.

Scientists and missionaries are rarely responsible for a massacre but they don't like to miss an opportunity. Oppenheimer tried to improve our understanding of the force and the seriousness of his science. He was compelled to seek its meaning. It was in Japan. His research was exemplary and his counsel insignificant. Napoleon brought ethnographers to Egypt to study the people he would slaughter. When we invaded the New World we dressed like pilgrims. We called the indigenous people Indians, just like in India. Their deaths have finally come to our attention. Just last week a Canadian Prime Minister apologized. It was a cruel age or a river that is always flowing. In Texas we embrace the new, but we never give it back.

The learned do away with the people they study by studying them. I am so bored with their humanity. I have killed a few and an aesthetician, but I'm not looking for praise, and this is not the war I'm fighting. I am speaking with a shortened tongue, not like the flames that lap and languish after a Texas visit. Everything that I have and have not said will bury me. This is just a starting point, true to its nullity and where I will persist. In this room I am learning the patience of paint and the wisdom of a Baltimore junkie. Hakim says there will be no time for despair while they're cutting off my head. I remind him that death comes after it is already gone and so it has nothing to do with me.

A few months after my arrival Aban and I were armoured and escorted to a city on the Persian Gulf. Texas had been there the day before, airing the place out from ten thousand feet. We set out with twenty soldiers to examine the efficacy of our penetration. On the beach there was a sprinkling of people, women and children mostly. Their clothes were too small for their bodies. Come swim they called to me, the tide rocking them gently to and fro so as not to disturb their sleep. All the while the local office was frantically inventing our success. To their credit, I used their words more or less as I found them. Texas is magnificent from a distance, up close we're Mississippi henchmen. Where are the men, I asked Aban. There, he said, pointing to the distant hills, watching.

As we were leaving Aban asked why these people had to die. They were smuggling babies into Nebraska, I explained ... what for ... Islamist sleeper cells ... I see. In New Orleans the ocean has settled its account and is on its way to L.A., Monsanto is boasting record yields on Wall Street where food sits unrecognizable, fomenting new disease to be sold as future worth to German pension funds. China is buying mountains one cargo ship at a time. In India a girl is mentoring her younger sister but she can't concentrate because her eyelid won't stop twitching. Now that the factory is gone, she explains, we'll go straight to whoring. We'll buy new dresses and then I'll teach you how to skip, your days and nights. What happens in Vegas is squalor in Bhopal.

Too many are speaking with my mouth, a bird, a mouse. When the world was flat I knew where not to step. Happiness, said Hakim, will come later. It must be true because when the head is severed the thoughts don't follow. But I'm not talking about a headless silence, I am already where I'm going and the coming ice age has my back. I'm talking about the decapitation of every Texas congregation, metaphorically speaking. We believe in war, a few per decade should keep things lively. It takes a massacre to keep the clicker on the coffee table, or footage of our boys shaving in the desert. Look honey, this doesn't look anything like Vietnam ... thank God, I am so tired of that young girl burning.

19

In Texas I sat on the front porch with a rifle and chewed tobacco, liberty was on my mind and eternity was on my side. Now it's over, or over there, riding horses and mending fences. From this room I resist the words that will remake the world. With a snap I am marking the outline of children running. I track a single gunshot. Soon I am dancing with squirrels, negotiating with a mouse and disagreeing with a bird. It seems I have forgotten nothing. I have told Hakim about Calabria, my mountain village, its hills plummeting into canyons. There the weak believe they will rise again, just like in Cuba or Madrid. In 1963 I took the first train out of town.

Today I'll be taken out to the courtyard but I will not be shot. Routines are important behind bars, reload, rewrite and then a nap. It's all too much but I'm learning to do nothing. During the night or in the early morning a peacock arrived and is strutting the perimeter of the courtyard. It's looking for a break in the wall but no one knows how it got in. Everyone is arguing about what it eats. I told Hakim I would ask the bird … what bird … he's from New York … really … he was sent by the Pentagon … oh … but he is stationed in Berlin … I see … he flies back and forth … of course … he can help … that's good … but he won't.

There are numbers growing on the tip of my tongue. Mossad keeps track of all the people who are and are not here but I don't think they know about the peacock. On January 1, 1948, David Ben Gurion said blowing up a house is not enough. We blow through one house to the next, opening the floor plan as we go. We are inside, outside the line of fire. Israel sold the technique to the Georgians now it's called The Georgia Rules. The customer is always right. Bird, what does a peacock eat … does it speak English … I don't think so … cooked rice and beans, raw vegetables, fruit and a little protein. I told Hakim. This is not New York, he said, the peacock is protein. I told the bird, he flew onto the windowsill and into the night. He was not amused.

Hakim and I have agreed on the peacock's diet and now we are discussing China. I take notes, and later I will rearrange what I said. China is just like Texas, he said, everybody looks the same except some people have more money. After Hakim leaves I move both chairs to the middle of the room, the table under the window facing the chairs. When there's no one here, there is so much more to do. In the morning this room will be in Tiananmen Square and I will give a speech, standing room only. I'll arrange these paragraphs end to end, frantically, because I have to reach Beijing by morning. In China there is a great silence under fluorescent lights, over rows and rows of workbenches. Unlike my speech, this is work that requires no explanation, all who apply can begin immediately. Hakim said this is how a billion people catch up with the rest of us.

As he was leaving, Hakim said it was not necessary to write down everything he said. The notes would never leave this room. I assumed he'd not been apprised of my trip to China. Too soon after his departure he returned, luckily the bird heard the key in the door and hid under the bed. Hakim handed me a handful of flowers, weeds mostly and a few petals, the greens are for eating, he said. Now I'm petal-struck. On the table my feathered comrade is reviewing everything that I have written. What are you doing, I asked … my job … what is your job … that's classified … I see … I'm recommending that we dispense with your services … why … you're having trouble sticking to one point of view … I can change that … is there anything you want me to report back to the President … tell him to send a double … you are the double … then replace the double … with whom … him … who … tomorrow he'll be in Beijing.

The dead from the last century have all been buried, now they are anonymous for good. Before the bird left to file his report he explained that Texas is the truth and so I have no reason to lament, no reason to exist. Then he handed me a letter from New York. I opened it. The woman who is my wife has asked for nothing. I do not have the nothing that she wants. From time to time I have spoken as though I will return. In New York I learned to walk myself around the block and wave as I passed by. It was the best that I could do. For a time I prowled the atlas, in every town the next town waited. I was trying to catch up with my story. I have not been home for many years.

Every morning Hakim brings me fruit, a little bread and jam, and each time I'm surprised. The food here is fine and death, so far, has been the death of others. My own will have no significance because I won't be there. Hakim will deal with the remains. The slow forward motion of a thousand caterpillars will fell a tree. Their work would be unbearable were it not resolved at birth, apportioned to the life of the other. In Texas everything is repeated and everything is true. I have explained to my captors that in Amarillo we blow cool air over empty beds, shoot blind horses and the nightingale sings just beyond the back porch. There are no terrorists there, just diabetes, heart disease and cancer. No one bleeds out in an afternoon.

At the onset of modernity I acquiesced to all accusation. This is what I said when they showed me the knife that would resist all grammar, I was there, I should have said something before and yes I can teach you to play the piano. It seems I do not coincide with my mind. I think, I am not, and ready to confess that I await my meaning or at least an expression with which to storm the castle. I have begged and bartered, bribed judges, consorted and cajoled but I never knew what to ask for. I realized too late there was nothing I wanted. I have explained this to Hakim, daily and in great detail in the hope that he would tell those charged with my execution. He said the soldiers stationed to this house are only attuned to the sound of emptying fluids and a few halted pleas.

In 1830, Algeria insulted the French consul and so France sent in thirty-four thousand troops. They stayed until 1962. After the Second World War the French were still eating rats, which were plentiful, and they ate what the Americans had in them to share. By the end of the decade the French were doing much better and then they remembered what they had forgotten about the sway of a skirt over the right pair of heels. Parisians who were not very good-looking moved to Algiers, but far from the shanty town and the medina. In 1861 Monet was a soldier in North Africa, that's where he learned about light. He observed that behind the sun the darkness collects in black quadrants of rampant death and carnival birth anywhere anytime. What the French know of colour will cut out your tongue.

Talk is cheap but it's better than running through the town screaming. Armies are ugly when they get bored, soldiers will amuse themselves with broomsticks, or broken glass. They adapt. After dinner some will commit suicide. Nothing has changed since De Gaulle visited our town. Mosquitoes still hover over stagnant water and from the abattoir young people are chosen to study in France, later sent back to ensure a lively debate. That shade of lipstick has not been seen here before. In Paris or Marseilles is where you'll find refinement, but you mustn't forget you're an Algerian. When you get home everyone will want to eat at your table, everyone will want to sleep in your bed. Make sure a machete is close at hand.

In the colonies, gatherings of two or more people are strictly forbidden, especially in basements. Anyone caught dreaming of April in January, of flour, more than ten ounces, will be dealt with severely, and no one will step in to take the blows in your place. Killing people one at a time is a good idea. It will not make the evening news but you will know, from your neighbour, you could be next. In Warsaw a priest is finding and recording the number of Jews that were killed by a single gunshot during the Second World War. No one knows why priests do what they do, not even priests, but it takes a long time to find a bullet in Poland. One, two and then tens of thousands in hundreds of places behind even bigger numbers and a mountain of soot.

I am moving forward, scouting ahead for safe passage. The light is gracious but too slow for the journey. I never sleep. I was born with an abnormally large head but it has not helped me at all, every morning I wake up with a headache. The poor will work for a smoke and a coffee, the swagger to keep them resolute during a prison stint, or get them through another winter. This is a style that is easily broken. What I am telling you now has not been invented. Perhaps I should carve these words into stone. One night I turned into a magpie, the night that I died. Amen and hallelujah. The mouse enters after the bird leaves for Berlin. First he will tell me everything, and then he will tell me the truth.

20

The vulture waits, it is an honest bird and prefers rodents to grasshoppers. I appear to be travelling again. In a truck filled with trade tools and a cavity large enough to conceal a body. Hakim is driving, one guard sits next to him and another in the back. I am in between. My eyes level with a sliver of light and a gun pointed inward. There is not enough space to move. Thoughts get interrupted, cut short by pain, lodge themselves in my vertebrae. Eggshells in between bone. I have been told that this will not be my last journey and nothing of our destination. A diminishing city suggests we are driving north. En route is the hastily discarded remainder of personal effects not yet fully picked over. But for a few carcasses the people have moved on, undoubtedly to better things.

From the roof of a forsaken building two men track this van kicking up dust as it zigzags to avoid potholes and abandoned vehicles. In the eye of a child of less than ten years the same van approaches. Hakim stops the truck, calls the child by his name and walks toward him. The boy stands in the pitiless sun amidst ribs of rust and garbage. Hakim picks him up and carries him into the shade. He lays a small canvas on the ground where he arranges food with careful instruction as to what to eat when. Patiently they go through it all again, unwrapping and rewrapping the next day's portions. He returns and puts the truck in gear. This is why we will kill you, he said.

On the road Hakim and the guards discuss this country's housing situation. A little house, says Hakim, it's not much to ask, beyond the reach of a superpower. The guard in the rear can hear him through the holes in my casing but not clearly enough to participate fully in the conversation. His contribution is not practical, just a few halted words. I hear both sides clearly, since it all has to go through my cage. If God has given us an opportunity, who are we to argue, said the guard in front. He's right, said the guard in the rear. The harder we work the less things change, said Hakim. He's right too. Things are different now, said the guard in front, for example that house over there. It's not much, a real fixer-upper and the previous owners we know will be reasonable as soon as we dig them out of the rubble. Right again.

On arrival the van is camouflaged in foothills and waiting. I am allowed to stretch. Hakim organizes the camp in caves augmented by tents that he pitches on a small blanket of sand in between rock. The guards clean their weapons. Hakim signals me to eat and queries the accuracy of his idiom. He calls me brother with much-improved diction. I awake to food spread over white linen, a picnic and a war. Like Bedouin my defenders situate themselves against the elements for bread and banter. We do not like Texas, said Hakim, and your President is imbecile. Your President is *an* imbecile. Your President is *an* imbecile? Good. Thank you brother, eat something. That night I couldn't believe my luck, my own little tent next to the van and only one ankle chained to the axle.

I am afraid in these hills, from sleepless night to dampened dawn, from greed to rust I wait. I was unacquainted with a scroll etched by shepherds and bleached into these stones long after my eyes shut. There is no reason between you and me, theatrics and a machine destined to repeat, an alibi and a list. Is it possible to die in another language? A beginning and then another where a traveller might wash his weary feet. In New York we lived in cliffs, glass and steel suddenly between the clouds. I set sail in a paper boat from the inside of a boardroom. In this desert botanists awaken Babylon in every spore, the myth and the law. Texas, I refuse to admit that for which I must answer. It's what I do, instead of everything else.

There has not been a spring like this before, so much death rising like smoke from a wasp's nest. We know nothing of what it is and when we do, it's a thousand years too late. Perhaps that's why we are so happy, and if we are unhappy it's for the same reason. I have this fury with which to tear the world. In New York we keep open scissors between the sheets amid dreams of decorating above the wind. A child born to these heights descends in a glass bubble. She is everywhere the body ends. She hears music all the way down. On the street a woman darkens her lips in a city where everybody dies twice because once is not enough.

In the desert the sky is always the same and there are no low-hanging branches from which to attach a rope. On the plus side, it takes fewer words to describe it. I sleep through the night, Hakim and the guards sleep in turn. From the inside of my tent the wind is comforting. When I understand it better I'll hitch a ride out of here. Texas soldiers are looking for the room where I had measured all the steps. The press secretary is anxious to announce my release; ladies and gentlemen we got him, or, mission accomplished. Anything to get him through the day's programming. In the meantime the President is not sleeping well. His vocal chords stretch and vibrate, muscular and gastric expulsions fill the emptiness, and some must die. He should never have been left alone with a sentence.

At the height of my popularity I have this waiting. I had a bed inside a jar, I still have a pencil but I have lost all the names. I can think, and that's what it takes to bring down the government. This place is fine for now, and for eternity. I have asked the bird and the mouse not to name the spot, what difference would one more marking make. Besides, I am already inside my apartness. We have brought provisions and our trifling notions to these caves. Hakim likes it when I talk about New York. I will resituate my death to have done with this voice, or whoever is speaking of books and a bicycle, of his dead mother. I am becoming a dying man. If I could be quiet the story would empty into the one who hears it. As for the dying itself, I am not able.

We have been here a week now, or a year. For dinner we trapped and cooked a lizard. I am adapting to these desert nights. We have our routines, left foot forward right foot lift. When in Rome, talk to the pigeons. All I ever wanted was power and a lot of money, my confession audible above the song of a single sparrow. The troposphere is my home, said the bird, you are but a speck beneath my wings. I told him he didn't exist and to hell with the bird. I want to be with you, Texas, to soar in your chariots above the clouds, deliver new and sudden beginnings to factory towns. I want to storm the border with a provisional authority and underwrite the disaster from a Dallas office in lockstep with a coalition that does not exist.

I awaken while being gagged, hooded and forced into the hidden cavity of the van. Hakim tells me they have spotted a platoon of Texas soldiers and there is not enough time to kill me. If I am discovered the soldiers will deliver my friends to a black room, fasten their balls to a wire, listen to what they have to say, and then shoot them. My protectors bury their weapons in the sand and begin a blessed descent from these hills to hail the new king. If they are not believed I will die here, slowly and in the dark. When I die will the trees hear my weeping, will the birds feel me kicking at this cage? I am already dust but for this broken story for which I will not be forgiven. I wish it were instead a spoonful of soup.

I will never wear sunglasses again. It has been night all day. The putrefied breath of my eyes inside a curtain, black moons in heat watching me, watching me. Listen to my plea, a different world, a different time where they do not burn the living. I could be quiet then and move to the suburbs for I am hungry for both life and death. What are we doing here, Texas, this country will always be somebody else's backyard. Perhaps we should have bombed San Francisco instead. They're not like the rest of us. There are only three men, bowels rumbling, who know where I am, send them back to me, Texas. I give you my word, before they kill me I will nail them to a figment and drown them in a notion.

I hear footsteps, my body wood and pain. Oh captors my captors what are the words. I will help you cut my throat with my tongue. Whoever wins possesses what is named, in the way of a name. Language *is*, always broken. There are three writers in one donut shop, this is a tough business. Tools are to be used and not seen. A missile in every pot, happier than the rest and archived to fix what is said later. Words went back and forth, that's how it is with air campaigns. I took an oath and worried I would not be found. Death is a word and the hydro bill went to the wrong address, there was a penalty. I am a man in a truck, that's how I know this is not the end. Hakim unties me, we go back now, he said. We *will* go back now. We *will* go back now? That's right. Thank you brother, drink something.

21

Hakim organizes our departure, in the distance a woman rummages after a sandstorm. She is sifting through sand, mining the contours for a piece of clothing or a note. Her spine is cast, shaped to recover her son's body. How many times can the same day begin again. There was a battle here, Hakim explains, from the air one could see people scatter like ants, only faster. On the ground nobody knew where anybody was, and then somebody brought in a bulldozer. Perhaps tomorrow there will be birth and no death, ashes at dawn and a summer rain, a paste in the back of the throat slowly eating the esophagus. The streets are filled with children who are not happy to be alive. They are waiting to march as one to the end of time. The sky is drawn in a yellow fog, the day is over and this is the end of time.

I remember so little of the Big Apple, the dull-eyed full-bellied fairy tale of his and hers everything, the beginning of a truly cosmopolitan epoch for budding aesthetes in black. In the eleventh century a physicist and philosopher named Ibn al-Haytham invented the camera in the port city of Basra. At the start of this millennium Texas destroyed all his books, cultural differences, explained a young man who studied philosophy at the university. Of the soldier from Tennessee who shot him with a tank he knew nothing. When I grew tired of Manhattan I'd visit Toronto. The people there have never been to Basra but Toronto is close to New York and that's good enough for that little town. There, in the gallery district, they will admire your tiny stunt.

I wanted to be nice, what to wear to the evening meal, the dog and I united in my humanity, but I had not learned to speak as I should. I have only this flimflam and if I am granted reprieve I will fly back to prepare the empire's collapse. I am not a spiritual man, that's why they won't let me live in a small town, a house, a yard and whatever fits in a shopping cart. In the spring I would stop and talk to Blanche in the parking lot. Her voice and mine agreeing on the war, better there than here, we'd say, and when will they fix the potholes. The killing has been relentless since Moses brought down the wrong word. I'm looking for a sky that will not crush us all. I will do my best to ignore my dream of Connecticut – silence like flesh like water, bodies everywhere.

Under no circumstance is the President symbolic. He *is*. That is, he exists in his unleashing. Thinking does not elevate him, or anyone. In Italy I kidnapped a suspect and sent him to Egypt to be tortured. The Italians objected and indicted thirteen Texas operatives. We secured the oil. Last night nothing happened. In Honduras I lived in a CIA post behind a Washington veto. I was sent to topple a priest and cause death or serious bodily harm to civilians or non-combatants with the purpose of intimidating a population or compelling a government or an international organization to do or abstain from doing any act. Definitions make really good jackhammers.

I have always hunted above the smoke. I am for and against murder, planned a life in which I am innocent. Death it seems will come from my executioner. My tongue finally still will steady my neck but I will never understand his inclinations, nor mine for that matter. What beast shall I adore, why am I alone. Surely these questions also belong to us. Perhaps you don't hear me speaking, Texas, outside this room buildings are still collapsing. I have asked the bird, the mouse and the messengers to report the body count because I understand the situation, Texas. You can't see a thing from ten thousand feet.

The allegation that some of us come back as lampshades was never proven. Eventually everything becomes more believable. But with the advent of directional lighting it's not worth pursuing, and the science was questionable. Besides, we still have Elvis, it's never too late to hail the King. He was in Memphis last week, and Jerry Lee Lewis is still talking to us with his fingers. Only the rest of us aren't real, cut-outs to which we can attach a number. But apparently we are part of a much larger story, still growing, that Texas will inherit because they have the machinery.

When I visited Aban's house he outlined the foundation to show me where the walls had been and then he asked me to imagine the chairs so we could sit and have tea. Texas, I am happy to be alive though it has come to nothing, nights, days and the occasional mistress. I am a proponent of what is not, as the first to arrive. Death makes the future possible, it is not here yet. If I could draw, there would be a cat on the bed and blood in the White House. When I leave this room you must dispose of the body or it will enter at will and close every door behind it. It will acquire the common sense of a criminal and speak with a frozen heart. I will be a threat to you after I'm gone.

The bird is an odd companion, without substance. I turned to face the window, it had perched itself on the sill. Ask me a question … what do you mean … ask me another one … why are you here … to assure you that I don't exist … I know that … then I am here to help you make sense of your delirium … you are my delirium, you're a dead bird from New York … don't complicate things … but you're not here … what difference does that make … you die with me … don't be daft … it's obvious … nothing is obvious … but you don't exist … we covered that … well … you're asking the future to show you where you are … and … and what … what do you have for me bird … nothing, you … nothing.

I have begun to survey a country for the dead. All roads lead to where we've been and heroes will be statues already. Without arms so they won't split their enemy, who in turn will be waiting and sizzling on a spit. Politicians too will be dead in advance, marble heads scattered to all manner of gardens. All legislation will require a pigeon's approval. We will, of course, dispatch a delegation to Texas as they are likely to continue to supply the largest complement of our citizenry. Their experience in this matter deserves every respect. The project is daunting but there are few exigencies that will concern the living. Namely how to stem the flood of bodies so we can better prepare for their arrival. We will in time adapt. We appreciate that Texas is the death that it makes, it is all future and want. It is the death of death.

The bird has begun to pace, its wings folded behind its back, head down, I feel a speech coming on, he said … really … pay attention … yes of course ... now it might be that the problematic existence of the constituent's particularity is a necessary affront to freedom and form and therefore hemorrhaging in the truth of the union by its singular, not yet festering, physicality. People it seems are either being born or dying. The question indicated and never examined is the hypothesis that guides our work in the dialectic between master and master. Populace-based change is a perennial flaw of democracy aborted with notable frequency in favour of autocracy, the true spirit of basic order and hunger to the people.

He mouthed a few more phrases, pleased, he continued. Fear is best to secure the disaster and our credibility as rogue agent of despair. We offer a declaration of magnificent intent. Exalted idiom is the requisite correlate to brutality and carries no information. Citizens are required to love with dread and a bolstering nod until the bombs rain, reign with considerable liberation and the cost of decades that might lead serious Switzerland to host a meeting of thirty countries or so to prepare for the advent of Texas' forewarned and devastating approach. We are the state, men born to violence, living in common, drunk on the king's kindness and his right to war.

Mr. President, I have no questions and you have no answers. Texas fights the wars the British can't afford. The world is calling you from the highest mountain, bring your surfboard, the forecast is melting. I wish to compliment you on anticipatory defence. It is perfect for small men like me. Kill whom you want, their terror is evil, ours does not exist. Brilliant. Russia is scuttling long-range warheads on an endless rail anticipating our next target. Chechen spies are collecting train schedules. Tormented youths with computers and no families are peeking into launch sequences, Texas in space on a hair-trigger. What fun, apocalypse soon, Mr. President, apocalypse soon.

22

This is a pickle on a string, nothing but the nothing, it is a severed head. I do not have an exit strategy. I appreciate the little things, blood in the urine, a Montreal bagel, the end of our conversation. I want to find salvation above a Manhattan restaurant and then fly to Milan for an espresso with Armani. I want to look good in a tan. I want to be forgiven by people in old photographs and then I'll forgive them. I want to think of something first. I want my doctor to predict my death after I die. I want my tongue to break. There is a corpse outside my window, stray dogs and one wild rose, a feast I do not understand. Hakim said the dead man sold information. I can't imagine what was so important.

When we annihilated the red man no one batted an eye, it meant nothing. These days anybody can get a fishing licence but the river decides who to talk to. The fish and the indigenous people still have a dream. We're not in it. The Mennonites now live where the buffalo roamed, they are a charitable, God-fearing bunch, and they also fear television. They send shovels to Laos and pencils to Cambodia. In Indochina we bombed schools and poisoned the bulls, now everybody pulls their own plough. In Nicaragua we fought the birth rate. We also invaded Guatemala, Korea, Guam, Samoa, the Philippines, Vietnam, Indonesia and Idaho, twice. When something is said something else needs to be said, I'm just trying to keep us up to date.

Texas wants the western hemisphere, the Far East, the former British Empire and everything else if possible. After they get it I'll rename this place Kansas. I've made a list of what is mine, it's in the shoebox underneath my bed. Each morning I check it, note what's there and all that's missing. Every day Aban and I went to work, such was our life together, trucks full of money and good conversation. At day's end I buttoned everything down with a few paragraphs. Aban made separate lists of those who took money, one for the record and another he pocketed in case they forgot. Then he read aloud my summation. Your notes are ridiculous, he said, and the rest you don't understand.

Doug Coe once told me the separation between church and state is a good idea and then he unleashed both. With God on our side we'll change the world, he said, but San Francisco we'll keep under surveillance. In Vietnam Eisenhower installed a Christian regime in a Buddhist nation, a few backroom manoeuvres followed by a massacre. The Air Force was outstanding but President Johnson just couldn't find the words to explain their accomplishments. Death fades, Doug assured the Commander-in-Chief, especially in the less important nations. Then he pulled out an atlas to mark where they weren't, yet. Incidentally, that's Haiti, he said, the next soft spot for communism, and the golf courses will be magnificent.

Special interest groups, namely the media, the people and the international community, are disagreeing with our foreign policy. During the Reagan years newspapers were over-reporting the administration's activity. It was clearly an excess of democracy. The press secretary pruned his dance card and the Vice President suggested better judgment and proxy. To Guatemala, Reagan dispatched Israeli commandos and Neo Nazis from Argentina. The London *Economist* wrote favourably of Israel's success. The Nazis were never there. The world is not very big and even smaller if you look at it from space without your binoculars. That's why Texas is working to cordon the sky, all that infinity is not on our side.

I am afraid but the stones beneath my feet are not moved by my lament. When they were mountains the sun waited respectfully and time stopped in the valley. The moment I was born I took this job. I inhabit a carnival space, chance sparks from the boiler room. When I close my eyes everything is still burning, but there's nothing I want. The revolution in Nicaragua was a communist conspiracy to take what belongs to us. Infant mortality fell, literacy was through the roof, they had to be stopped. In 1854 the town of San Juan Del Norte levied port charges against the yacht of Cornelius Vanderbilt. The American Navy torched the town to the ground but that was a long time ago. Only the immediate is unbearable.

Do the Texas messengers see me or the one instead of me who speaks for both of us. Who will say that we were here when there is no one left. I will think more on this and then submit my report. Have you been talking to the guards, they ask … no … why not … they won't talk to me … who have you talked to … Hakim … who is Hakim … an orderly, someone who works here … what have you told him … that we separate fathers from children and consign both to eternity … what did he say … he already knew … what else … he knows what we did in Nicaragua … and … he says the papers here are reporting all casualties … anything else … everybody wants us to leave … have we polled the population … we stopped polling in 1993 … why … we were getting the wrong answers.

Hakim is back and he's asking about the empire's early days. When the English first came to New York, I begin, illiterate parasites and pariahs, there was plenty of room to swing an axe and no cafés ... oh ... they spent the first winter boiling each other and dreaming of the great white hope ... when was that ... we know it was January because broccoli was so expensive ... I see ... when the weather finally broke we built better shelter and the Cherokee gave us seeds ... that was nice of them ... then we suggested they leave so we could plant them ... then what happened ... they were confused so we explained private property ... I see ... and God's will ... which was ... the red man would move to Kansas and we didn't have to be English anymore ... I see ... but God was only half right ... oh ... Kansas was ours too.

Hakim understands everything I say, prisoners in this room have a way of speaking, he explains, please continue ... at the turn of the nineteenth century I was with Andrew Jackson in a Nashville tavern. He was shot protecting his wife's honour. She slept around or she was just flirtatious, history is not clear on the subject. Such rumours are common in Tennessee and a family tradition because they often include your sister ... I see

... by 1812 he had more or less recovered from his wounds, he took command of the American forces and went off to fight the British ... then what happened ... he won and rewarded his President with thirty million acres from the Creek nation and a few million from his allies, the Cherokee.

I like numbers, said Hakim ... in 1829, Jackson was elected President on a platform to dispose of the Indian problem. He and Joseph Smith believed that the continent once belonged to a superior race which had been wiped out by the existing savages ... who is Joseph Smith ... he was the founder of the Mormon religion and an epileptic ... was Andrew Jackson an epileptic ... no he was a Scottish Presbyterian. In 1829, the adult literacy rate among the Cherokee nation was higher than that of the union, and a white woman married a Cherokee man ... oh dear ... Connecticut burned them both in effigy and destroyed the Cherokee printing press ... why did they do that ... the Indians weren't ready for civilization.

In 1830, Congress passed the *Indian Removal Act*. Davey Crocket objected and Joseph Smith told his flock the Garden of Eden was in Missouri ... who is Davey Crocket ... a hero in a fur hat ... I see ... by 1838, most of the Cherokee had been rounded up and put in stockades. They were not murdered, they died from hunger and disease to make room for what God intended ... oh ... but nobody noticed because the radio had not yet been invented ... I see ... Jackson eventually died but we know he's living in the hereafter because on the reservation they still feel his boot on their neck. By the end of the century cotton had exhausted the land, nothing would grow except peanuts. In 1955, Jimmy Carter seized an opportunity.

All I want in this creation
Is a pretty little wife and a big plantation
Way up in the Cherokee Nation.

Will you teach me that song ... it's a jingle, singing it will make you glad ... what happened next ... the Russians sent a few monkeys into space but the monkeys never told anybody what they saw ... why not ... they were sent against their will ... I see, what else ... everything changed in Missouri ... oh ... you have to be invited to a funeral now, songs and light refreshments usher in eternity and a few close friends ... your country is very interesting ... tomorrow I will tell you how we conquered Mexico and gave some of it back ... tell me now ... I need to review my notes ... I see ... the numbers too ... of course ... go now and practice the jingle.

23

One morning I looked in the mirror and looking back was a stranger. He was hastily arranging fragments, a facsimile of an image but I could see no resemblance. What have you done, I asked, with my reflection. No answer. On the tip of my toes and with great speed I rounded the glass from the other side. I found the rascal in the middle of nowhere which, coincidently, was very nearby, a swamp, just behind my eye. We discussed the reason for his disengagement. My predicament as your reflection is racked with insufficiency, he said, I'm tired of the rupture, when you don't see me I cease to be. I want to exist beyond your appearing. Tomorrow I'll bake a cake, I said, and you can lick the spoon. Every morning he asks if it's tomorrow, and every morning I tell him not yet. Things are no different now but at least we are together again, and in the same room.

In the late morning Hakim brought me olives and bread. Eat, he said, and then we'll go out … out where … to the town square … will I be killed … no … why, then … a visitor is coming … and he wants to meet me … not exactly … oh … he is here to recruit and the people take heart in your capture … I see … I'll come back for you when the time comes. It's cozy in my room and I delight in the detail, the hint this house was once a mansion. The ceiling height, for example, I take comfort in the fact that my feet will not hit the ground. This was the servant's kitchen, Hakim explained, that's why its walls are mainly below grade and why it makes such a good prison. It would take an air strike to break through these foundations but, Texas, wait for my signal.

From the other side of the door I hear rattling, steel or cast iron. Hakim is back, just as he promised. We are going out but we're not going dancing. Between the two of us we have one son, we had two but one is dead and the other, as far as I know, is living in Iowa. He chains my feet to my hands, I can walk but not run just like the boys in Guantanamo. It's not what I expected but with chains on my ankles I can still think, it's what happens before the mouth opens. Then it's just talk, more talk and where the hell is my gun. Speaking of guns, there are two at the door in the hands of my keepers. They stand on the clear side of atrocity, on the upright side of murder, their backs are to a wall that has been there for hundreds of years, but I swear it was not there a moment ago.

On leaving Hakim confirms there will be no dancing. In the square I sit in the sun next to an improvised stage. The people stream by in the heat. Hakim stands next to me ladling water. An old woman picks up one cup for herself and one for her grandson. She asks Hakim if I speak their language. Yes. Why have you come here, she asks … I was ordered to come … you should have refused … I agree … I had six children and I could have had six more, four are dead and two are still fighting … I'm sorry ... your culture is a day old and an eggplant knows more than you do. Hakim whispers in my ear, she is very wise, a professor at the university, as he gives her water. She's right, he said, eggplants have been here a long time and they will be here long after we kill you. The woman returns the cups to Hakim but she is looking at me. You're a comma in these parts, she said, a comma on the banks of the Nile.

The man we have come to see approaches the stage, tall, with plenty of facial hair, traditional garb and a sidearm. To a predator drone he's Osama Bin Laden. Next to him are two guards with machine guns, several more line the perimeter of the square. An assistant sets up a microphone on the makeshift platform. The speaker now faces the people, behind them are tables adorned with mountains of food, mostly meat. Behind the tables is a brand spankin' new Hummer from Detroit. The previous driver is flush with cash, or he's dead. The people have eaten but they will eat again after the visitors leave. This war has been raging since we first cut a path in these hills, the man begins, with no reprieve to wash the blood from these stones. It kills without pity or anger. It is smaller than the misery it brings, bigger than the peace that will follow. In Texas it fits in a sound bite.

Hakim tells me that he has heard this speech before, he likes it but he's having trouble concentrating. He wants me to talk about New York. I search the skies for the drone, I fear this gathering will not go undetected for long. In New York the moon is still new, I begin, but everyone there pretends they're in Paris. People only talk to the living, they call this conversation. The men mimic George Clooney and so do the women, together they drown in a puddle. In New York a man will follow a woman in a good pair of pumps from India or China. Countries that are neither here nor there but on the other side of some ocean, the murmur of a few billion people that work while we sleep until they board a canoe for Seattle. Hakim listens carefully to the things I say and assures me no one will kill me today. When this is over, he said, we'll go back to your room and talk about whatever you want, but I hope it's Detroit.

In Detroit the glass towers empty at five o'clock and all the white horses head for the thoroughfares. When they are not at the office they're golfing in China. On Sunday the people without cars form lines under steeples. Churches have heat and everything seems easier when you're in the choir. In Detroit you don't need an address to take delivery for what the day brings, unless it's a government cheque. Dare to dream, is what the preacher said, and if you're not happy you're not dreaming hard enough. Someday we'll have dishes to wash and go back to a time when our veins weren't collapsing. No one remembers the time that he's talking about. Dream, he says, that behind every church there's a factory and behind every factory a parking lot instead of a ditch. Smoke rising from thousands of chimneys, black and witless molecules from New York to L.A., with nothing left for them to turn into.

Back in the square the speaker is calling himself a general. He is addressing the crowd from a stage built from lumber that just a few days ago might have been a table. Or a wall so goats could tell the yard from the house. The general enlivens everyone's penchant for murder, helps farmers abandon their crops and their young. I know because I used to do his job. Numbers and bullshit in the same sentence. What he says and what he refuses to say is the same. A satellite cannot see your tears, he exclaims, and the people who operate the equipment have never known fear. Everyone is fed up and to the general it doesn't matter with what. The future is a spike he'll nail to their forehead. Bullets then ballots is what he's suggesting, and this time, he says, we promise to count them.

Before the speech ended Hakim stuffed his bag full of meat, some bread and two cans of Campbell's soup. They're headquartered in Jersey, for directions check the internet. The general had so much to say but this is not it. I'm telling you what I heard. He and his entourage drove several times around the square and then through the town. Each jeep had two flags, one for the province, though they were not from here, and one for the nation. The general rode in the Hummer. He stopped from time to time and stood on the hood. He was regarding things from afar and watching for those who quickened their pace. The warden is new and the prison eternal, he came to increase his inventory and I knew that he knew, everyone loves a parade.

Hakim and I are tearing through bone and through ligament. We're keeping the party going and the general, we've agreed, should move to Siberia. My room is a boat, a hut in the desert. The thing adrift marks the beginning of my astonishment. It is torn from the miracle. In 1971, I was in Indonesia to help organize their first prayer breakfast in celebration of the 1966 decree by which Suharto seized power and commenced to slaughter. There is no authority but God, and bankers. I explained to Hakim it was not my intention to complicate matters. Texas disagrees with, but will defend to the death, the things that I'm saying. I was young and likely drunk when I capitulated. In Texas freedom is fatal.

I could say more of what happened in the square and the bird will want a report. Some will die, on this we'll agree, and the things that remain, bones and two empty soup cans. In the morning I will examine them closely, check the labels for messages. This is work best done in daylight. Of the speaker who turned into a general I could say he had prisoners hidden in towns all over this land but none as important as me. He might have said that my death would send a shiver through tides and through time, it would hang for eternity by a thread between the earth and the moon. But he didn't. I could say the old woman came back and that her grandson spit in my general direction. But I won't.

Allow me to explain. Death is a just formality and from where I begin. Let's assume for the moment that I occupy a frame, this room made to order, equidistant between the walls that rise to support the beam from which I am hanging. More or less at the end of my work, and after Hakim has supplied me the rope, in this, my new life, the beginning. Nothing follows death and it's better than heaven because it exists. Nothing is a lot. When a tourist takes a photograph of a New York tower the structure is not represented, what she sees does nothing to stop it from falling. What is at stake is the space before which the doors and the windows are hung. Inside this space is where we work to produce the assumption that there is such a thing.

Before I was captured and before Aban arrived each morning with my tea and biscuits I awoke to the sound of construction. Soldiers and labourers were assembling barracks at a distance measured beyond the throw of, say, a five-pound bomb from the other side of the compound wall. The sergeant in charge was a Mormon and he ran the site like a Missouri barn-raising. Beyond the barracks, but on this side of the brink, were the locals we'd hired to help win the war. They were between us and that bomb that I mentioned earlier. The modules they assembled did in fact resemble long miniature barns. We have many factories that produce such things, said Aban, this does not seem efficient. The Vice President and his friends own the factory, I explained. Loyalty is very important, he said.

When it was not the hammering that woke me it was a rooster crowing from a small yard adjacent to the construction. He announced his waking, no doubt, after he'd stepped out of the shower. Roosters rise early and so they never need to scramble for a train but they will do nothing to help win the war. They don't attend meetings and each time they're assigned a task they claim to be guarding the henhouse. During one of the gulf wars, I can't remember which, my mission was to investigate roosters and their affiliates north of the thirty-fifth parallel. Southern roosters are much more patriotic. What I found was alarming. What a rooster knows is that he's of no use to anyone dead so long as there's a hen around in a nice pair of shoes.

In Texas I had the President's ear and he signed immediately my decree to intern the roosters. This is a program that had worked well before, recently with the yellow man and before that, the Cherokee. Then the President and I discussed baseball and sultry Manhattan. He had his limits and favourite topics of conversation. His press secretary gave me the list. It did not include situations like this, perhaps that's why he doesn't answer my letters. Life drags on, habit interrupted by terror, or the other way around. I can't sleep, is what I wrote to the Commander-in-Chief, but the words felt like someone else's and from this room the moon looks like a skull.

24

What we learned at Auschwitz is that if you hand someone a bar of soap they'll do the rest. Soap was the first thing Hakim brought me but I wasn't worried because he also brought water. In this country hygiene is important, but it's just hygiene. Then he listened for days and weeks or perhaps it was just a few hours. My advice to you, said Hakim, is find a higher power. I told him the difference between God and a muddle had not been invented and the muddle, I suspect, is much more important. As for those who come and go – the bird, the mouse and the Texas messengers – they don't exist, merely persist. I can't rely on their counsel. Hakim is the exception, he brings food and keeps me company. When I unload my head he leaves in a wobble. I worry he won't come back but every day he brings something, nuts or kiwi. At all other times I wait for the universe to empty.

When my son left home I walked him to the curb. That's the way to China, I said, and so is the other way but it takes longer … I see … now go, don't stop and don't get stuck in what might have been … you said birds would teach me to fly and squirrels waited for me to run in the park, you said the words were for dancing … that was before, from now on joy must have a reason … I can't live in this place … when you were not in the park squirrels hid their food and prepared for disaster. Like camels with a rope through our nose is how we built the cities. All I know is this detour, this blend of hilarity and horror. Things will be better when you get to China, or worse. I'll send you a postcard, he said, from a cornfield in butt-fuck Iowa.

As soon as I was captured I understood that my son would be fine and then I outgrew the rest of my problems. Hakim suggested I send the boy a letter to let him know things just get better. I'll do it tonight, I said, postpone work on my book. Besides, it's getting monotonous and all this twisted carnage is not very interesting. When the mind threatens I close my eyes, death, obviously, is not the last word. They are so messy, the newly slain, not at all like in Hollywood. The details pertaining to slaughter make for lousy writing and even worse footage. In the letter I wrote to my son I told him to renew his interest in squirrels. Flying, I said, much to my surprise was in fact possible, but I wouldn't recommend it.

When we started this war the state department had no idea that the weapons that did not exist would go missing. Then I was called to the Capital. The President instructed me to keep an eye on Rumsfeld, who told me to watch Dick. Dick said we didn't have to worry about Powell or his visits to the Oval Office. He just wanted to talk about his tanks in the desert. Condoleezza liked him but what she liked more was playing the piano. She played for the Queen. Blair attended her performance at the palace. For old times' sake he briefed her majesty. India, he said, is no longer yours. Then Tony told everyone a funny story about a one-legged terrorist. You have to tell that story again, Condi said, at my recital with Yo-Yo Ma.

The planning dragged on, first we built a wall and then we went in. Information is power, said Condi, so I never take notes. Our job, she explained, is to win the war and structure the peace that will follow. I know now, that was the last time I would never learn to play the piano. I took a room in a country nearby and for a while I was comfortable until the enemy fired on the hotel. Then I went around the region building runways, Tommy Franks and his wife needed places to land. I negotiated with governments and generals who would have preferred to shoot them out of the sky. From time to time I went back to New York but with my son gone there was no reason to stay. Now I'm a prisoner. As for the rest, it never happened, at least that's how I've decided to tell it.

I'm covering ground like a hunted gazelle but I always come back to the same story – death. My voice reminds me of where I've been. In Miami they say Jesus rose and fell, or the other way around, to forgive our misshapen lives. We're living forever because someone thought to plant him for a few days in the sun. That guy works for us now. Bill or Harry from Kentucky has a health plan and a company car. He works in Guantanamo and some other places that are neither here nor there. I used to build crosses in Galilee, he said. I helped Jesus confess to things he'd not seen and places he'd never been. A hasty script and a scrawl with all but a few broken fingers. With two kids in braces, a mortgage and a TV that keeps getting bigger, there's just no time to build crosses anymore.

Hakim is struggling to learn English, more words to augment our omission. Brooks also babble, without presumption and they don't have a choice. The beam from which I will hang myself is still here, thankfully. In this country buildings are the first things to go. I'm the smartest guy in the room when the mouse isn't here. The war, it seems, has gotten much smaller. The rodent hangs on my every word, but if I turn to look, he disappears. Into thin air or a restaurant perhaps, some place that's not on this page. Still, every day we make plans. Nothing, we agree, must be left to chance and he says I can rely on his reporting of my final twitch. I, in turn, will testify that he was there.

We must hurry, said the mouse … why … you can't be killed if you're already dead … I need a little more time … for what … to think … about what … dying … you think of nothing else … thinking and dying are not the same thing … are you sure … no … you're dragging your feet … what if I were to jump from the Brooklyn Bridge, it's a popular spot … that's no longer an option ... do something mouse … like what … an intervention … a what … from Texas … they don't know where you are … maybe the executioner will change his mind, see the light … he's seen it … and ... and what ... has he made sense of it … he's says you're the object ... of what ... your disappearing … what's the subject … what you are not … is he sure … no … what about my story … you call this a story … what's wrong with it … everybody sounds the same.

The mouse, the bird and I have had occasion to disagree. It is unlikely we will see eye to eye on a subject as important as me. In Texas I would have by now cocked my double-barrel, inhaled a little sulphur and have done with the pesky rodent. As for the bird, he's already dead. Absence is but one aspect of my duration, small comfort for a small man. In New York too I would routinely go missing, though I never reported it. I disappeared inside that book I didn't understand in high school, full of unusual and refractory thought. It was written by William Burroughs, the last cockroach in Manhattan who didn't move to Jersey. Daily I brought it and my wife to the café. I wanted to conquer the world to be rid of it, and the book was a perfect size to keep the sun from my eyes.

The bird is pacing the length of the table again, he's looking to improve on a threat. The mouse thinks I should die now, I said … the mouse is an ingrate and you are under contract … I see … you have to finish the story … what story … any story … I've forgotten everything … that's the one … I'm making it up … you got it … I refuse … exactly … what is this, bird … it's nothing … is it necessary … it distracts us … from what … we don't know … who's we … I can't say … will I be here long … what do you mean … how long is my contract with Texas … you have no contract with Texas … who is my contract with … that's confidential … who do you represent … that's classified … for how long will I have to work … what a question … will I ever be able to play the piano … no … maybe the mouse is right … he's not.

The bird should have stayed in New York. By 1898 we were done with the Indian problem. The President asked God if we should next take the Philippines. Get it while you can was the answer. McKinley sent in sixty thousand troops. Our shelves are now full to the brim with everything that country produces. Power is ordained, McKinley explained, and where the army sleeps, we'll call that Jerusalem. As for the rest, we have His promise, no pain in eternity, and Manila can just build more churches. That war is over now, lesson learned, bypass the legions, go straight to surveillance and plenty of operatives. We'll call that plan A. Plan B is a raging inferno and the last resort because we lose too many customers.

Doug Coe never invited dictators to his prayer meetings, they came, and like Jesus and Lady Liberty he turned no one away. Give us your tired and your poor but those with whom we can do business will never sleep under bridges. The Bible is full of mass murderers, he explained, they're good with detail. There are people who live all their lives in the same room and then, before I can find an apt metaphor, they're salivating at the Mexican border. In their pocket is the flyer from that awful night when we delivered them their freedom. Texas forgot to specify who to surrender to or the time of the last transport, but how lovely is the picture of the Washington Monument. They come for the dream, adrift in backwater Mississippi.

25

Before my capture we pulled the best minds from the ruins and everyone who agreed with us had a place at the table. Legislators, judges and generals were anxious to begin work on the new constitution. We met in the palace and Rumsfeld kept busy smashing tongues, a slagheap of words but none from the rubble. When I drafted the directive that warrants would not be made requisite to search the houses still standing, the new fathers protested. If we allow Texas to enter at will, they reasoned, the people will not have rights, they will not have freedom. I explained exigent circumstances. Just like before, said the new minister of justice, everyone will understand.

Hakim is sitting on a mat he brought with him, that's what he does when he plans to stay. Today he needs me to speak for the President. I focus while pacing the length of the room, he sits perfectly still. Between the door and the window I could lose everything. The President is bigger than this house, I begin, we are skewered from the cradle to play for the home team. In Texas we eat with a fork, in other places it's chopsticks, but your best plan is hunger, Hakim. This is the same old story, he protests, what of the promise of a woman's shoulder, weekends on the open road, death in a trailer park. We are so similar with our cocks and our guns, quickly to the end of time. That was the last century, I explain, in New York we have new pastimes. Colonics and cholesterol, the morning run and art, provided it is not too depressing.

It is good to be a horse, coursing through leaves and through water. At the first opportunity I will gallop to the nearest mountain and wait. I won't be the first. I am attached to my loathing and someday I'll weep, but for now this thought is too big for my ears, too big for my faces. Soon I will begin work on a hole back to Texas. The day that I died was like any other, like today for example or yesterday. A day from which I will not return. Terror grows and sometimes I confuse it with greatness, both, I think, are someone else's.

When I come down from that mountain or climb out of this hole, everyone will see the distant is near. I'm doing all I can with this nothing, but I need the name of that horse.

It is best if we do not go back to the village. Everyone is sleeping forever and in London they're only reporting the weather. An English drizzle, planes over burning water and clearing instantly a school in mid-sentence. If you fly for England you don't need an alibi, no one on our side believes the rumours. Still, we should be discreet. Al Qaeda takes the tube with your sister. I keep my brain under my hat, but it won't stop a bullet and that's all that stands between me and Bin Laden. Yesterday God and I agreed on the shoes, a sensible pair. He's always been there for me, like the bird, the mouse, or a fly in July. You are but the trifling sum of your body parts, he said, but a quality shoe will outlast a kidney.

In the eye of a one-eyed dog this country has not yet fallen. Flies in an empty socket, the chance limbs of its former deities and, on occasion, a little meat on the bone. Dogs never hanker for a rope and beam. They don't presume. With every air strike the view of this place from space just gets better and Texas never cared much for the architecture. We see all there is to see of that dog and his encounters, but everyone who lives here wishes he still had his privacy. This country is beginning to look a lot like Vietnam. From the bottom of a ditch a severed foot has understood its condition, but it doesn't know which brain to complain to and the trucks that clean up the mess are not equipped for DNA testing.

The best cure for art is death. A stillness adequate to its failure and finally, an end to the whimper. There's no difference between breasts and the Himalayas except the mountains have been speechless for longer. I grow old, I grow old, words to usher in the absence of everything. I left her standing in the doorway, but others continued to walk past her window that afternoon and then a year. Rain helped her discover the feelings of a woman waiting. When we were together we took turns speaking the thing that was never said. I've since learned to talk to a dead bird and a mouse. Soon I will refuse to speak with a fly. It never occurred to me to learn the squalid speech of a one-eyed dog still hoping to mount the endless orgasm.

I am dying with laughter. Al-Khiam is an Israeli torture chamber in Lebanon administered by mercenaries and Special Forces. There, bombs are sold at bargain rates with an excellent maximum kill per hit to dollar ratio. When people vote for consumption we all win. A butterfly is too fragile to be bronzed and so it transitions quickly to its nonexistence. I was at the Temple Mount when Ehud Barak secured the freedom to worship for all with flying gunships. A few days after that romp, William Jefferson Clinton born William Jefferson Blythe III made the largest sale in a decade of Cobra and Apache helicopters. Israel also bought the extended warranty and all the spare parts Bill had lying around. *The Caribou County Sun* of Soda Springs, Idaho with a Thursday circulation of 2,813 did not report the sale.

It is impractical to manufacture major weapons systems in Israel and transactions between democracies do not permit stipulation. We cannot second-guess every commander who calls in an air strike. *The New York Times* will be unable to tally the missing, subject as they are to interpretation by prodigious intellectuals, some of them French. In France they drink to the happiness of man and the poor go to bed early. Our story cannot be breached in or out of Albuquerque. Texas, what's taking you so long, I'm a captive but can't you see I'm still free? This is no time for restraint and I know, from our work together, there is no such thing. The secret of taking, Rumsfeld told Dick, is a massacre and a story, or the other way around. Dick told George, George told Tony, Tony told the Queen. Go and see if I am over there said the Queen.

Soon after the Oslo accords construction began on a barrier to encircle the Palestinian population. But it didn't matter because there was no country behind the wall. Just children who can outrun a rocket with or without a hole in their shoe. When the infant first opens its mouth it is its final plea. After he dies we will know him as Muhammad al-Durra. He is standing in Little Rock Arkansas, staring down the barrels of an Apache helicopter, a slingshot in one hand and the ring of his dead father in the other. He has come with his name and his weapons to die again in this nothing place. Don't touch me, he says, because you could not, because you would not know what you were touching, because I could not bear it.

In Texas the same is not the same as the same, it is the dispensation of immensity. Slaughter is built on repetition. In September, when buildings fall, New York looks like Baghdad. So does Baghdad. I have abandoned my plans to assassinate the President before he next takes the oath. A corpse is just a corpse, regardless of status or the country it comes from. The people here wait for the sky to fall but they're hoping for a better life at the end of a spoon. Both would put an end to the screaming. Unlike a cluster bomb that's not fully exploded. Bomblets, or sub-munitions, they look just like baseballs. Children are partial to the things they can't have, it's natural, and it's nothing really. A little more nothing and they'll have seen everything.

When I had feet I travelled with great haste to restaurants and barbershops with my no-nonsense genitals. I was in Kyoto when Texas announced that they were opting out of the weather. It's not good for the economy, Greenspan explained, and when disaster hits we'll just make more money. The decision strengthened the President's popularity in Marietta, Mississippi which had no registered sex offenders as of July 2007. In Marietta only the air has no colour, and they don't mind murder but spare them the details. It's too hot. In the summer chickens catch up on their sleep, no one in their right mind would turn on a fryer, and who cares about the news from Japan. Here, everyone waits for the climate to change, and honey, said Orville to his wife Matilda, the President is from Texas.

The messengers are back and they want information. From now on we will visit less and when we're not here we'll talk telepathically ... just like twitter, or is it jitter ... something like that ... but from the inside of my head ... that's right ... does the government know about this ... of course ... is the language dying ... we're not sure ... find out ... we need to see your files ... they're in New York and I can't remember what's in them ... try ... I can invent something ... fine ... let's begin ... let's ... I was happier then ... your personal story is not our concern ... but that's all I have ... go on ... I had no idea that I would live out my days as a lodger ... get to the files ... I'm setting the scene ... a little less detail please ... I have to tell the story ... who says ... the editor ... stick to the facts ... these are the facts ... I think you're missing the point ... that is the point.

In my room I divide my time between sleeping and dying, too much and too little but I never know which is what. I'm relying on the luck of the universe, snake eyes and a different train every time. That's why I can never find myself in it. There's no limit to the places I've been. Hence so many towns will not be named, Disa and Birmaza of Darfur, for example. What we do not see will grow, gluttony in the eye of a camera, the world focused on a body starving and infected with lice. Soon mountains will nail themselves to the sun. The wind will scream through burnt canyons and open onto a tomb filled with stagnant water, the archive. Dumb as rain.

There are hands to conceal the shape of clay. There are brushes to paint our eyes shut. There are books that will never be read and you can't tell a king by his photograph. I tried to tell my story to a mouse and a dead bird but they fell asleep. I am alone in a room and my hair feels like barbed wire. I have been found guilty of murder, women and children mostly. Conversations I have with myself should not be encouraged, three cheers for the things that I'll never say. In Africa I represented the World Diamond Council. When I returned from the field I gave seminars to the membership. I showed them picture after picture and a mountain of bones. And then I showed them how to act surprised.

26

Before we invaded this country the President spoke to his commanders in the field. We are the truth, our mission sublime, he began, I read it in the statement I signed yesterday. Last century, phones were phones and cameras were cameras. Everywhere was far and we were free to do what we do. Tell the embedded correspondents it is important that we have comprehensive and transparent reporting of the welcome and the merriment that will coincide with our arrival. All copy should be written in advance. Fiddling and thighs aflutter is how we'll usher in the war, said the President, and finish it. As for the stars and the moon, we'll turn them back on again during the celebration and then for a few hours each evening. At all other times everyone can write letters to their steady, but if she's a he don't tell the Army.

After meeting with his commanders the President met with media moguls over dinner and some fine Scotch. I started this conflict, he said, it's up to you to decide its meaning. Let's not forget the final solution was a media success before they built the death camps. Make sure your editors know, no corpses and no photographs of those who have begun, but are not finished dying. War is a catastrophe and it's abstract. Not for us to understand. These are the Texas arts that mark better days to come. Remember, he added, there are six of you and six is still too many. Before the President left they finished off the bottle. Six, sighed Rupert Murdoch, will only make the message stronger. Let's open another bottle, said the bigwig from Time Warner, and practice disagreeing. Let's get this story straight.

The future is garbage and a bargain at ten times the price. We send scrap metal to Bangladesh, electronic waste to Ghana while plastic forms a noose at the equator. On the steps of the Kremlin Yeltsin put a flower inside the barrel of a tank that sealed the fate of Gorbachev. Then he went looking for the highest bidder. I was there. So was the IMF, the World Bank and some other people who were not formally introduced. We helped dismantle the union, administered the shock, and the therapy. The worst gives rise to the best of opportunities. The Russian people are finally free to express their newfound hunger. But this is not my concern and much bigger than the things that I'm saying. In New York I used whiskey to backfill the holes inside my brain but in the morning they opened up again, and I had to squint to keep the buildings in Manhattan from melting.

Hakim is done with his language lesson and he's asking about Mexico. Mexicans no longer complain about the Spaniards, I begin, those heady days when Cortez filled his ships and took an interest in Aztec anatomy. There's less gold now but nobody cares because currency is just a multiple, the underlying does not exist. In the new economy Mexico buys guns from Texas with dollars from L.A. and Baltimore. In Bel Air they can't tell the worm from the hook since they catch their fish in a restaurant. They pay good money for a pig in a poke, but sometimes the pig is just baking soda. In Baltimore it's more of a volume business, no bricks and mortar just kids on the corner to keep the overhead low. If they run out of product they'll still take your money. Mexicans understand markets and demographics. Where they go, Wal-Mart follows.

Texas television never goes down. They flog the red, white and blue because the other colours don't matter. At Christmas there's no snow to smooth out the view, but there's plenty of kin to holler in the New Year. Hakim listens to everything I say. Many will die but in Texas they just change the channel, and on the Lord's birthday they'll call a ceasefire. Hakim sees his own blood in these blessed fragments, in the curiosity of a knife, a bullet deaf in a sandstorm. But this is not how he'll die. Death does not take place where it takes place. It is stirred into the lemonade and the step of a marching band on Main Street. Death as remedy, as means, the accrual of an alibi reborn. Death is dreamed behind the walls of a Texas steeple.

Hakim told me he killed his dog so that it would not lead the soldiers back to his family. This country is ending, he said.

I don't know why he tells me these things. I suppose he wants me to know something of the man who is speaking. I told him yesterday I had visitors from Texas … really … sometimes I talk to a mouse … oh … and a dead bird … I see … but not at the same time … of course … they don't like each other … naturally … it makes sense then … yes of course … good … eat something brother … thank you. I have a pen and Hakim brings me writing paper. There are words everywhere and I am disagreeing with all that I'm thinking, and with God, when he arrives unannounced. All I need to know is who sent him.

Beethoven wrote the notes between his ears, he never heard a peep outside the ringing. The interval, he thought, there can be no greater freedom. Everything is, because it disappears – numbers, beats and measures. This is how he received the mountains, bone and snow. This is how the sun fits inside a radio. When I got here my face was waiting for me like a gap. When I pray, the words can't get past the ceiling, the few that do don't mean anything. Perhaps the silence isn't big enough. I can wait. Texas reaches behind borders, nouns and predicates, it finds the words it needs. This speaks to their understanding of the particular. It seems I no longer coincide with their point of view and so they have asked me to forget. Forget what ... everything ... I'll think about it.

Secretly I longed for a regiment, generations of offspring and a machine gun in every window. I had a wife, so far well and good. She paraded me on the back of a donkey as though I had a way of making myself understood. I trimmed my eyebrows to look like I was thinking and my mouth took to greeting everyone. Have you been to Pompeii, everyone is so peaceful there and it's always the middle of the day. My wife kept her head in Paris but, lucky for me, her thighs were still in our New York brownstone. You must work, she said, we will not speak of the consequences. Let's go and see again that nothing has happened, I suggested, the years to come are already a waste of time. Then I fed her peaches to disguise the days that were growing like tumours on her lips.

Falling ordinance and the sun are heating up the courtyard, the peacock takes cover in plain view. When the time comes he'll be easy to catch. I hide under the table, move to the window in between explosions. Everywhere I touch the beginning. The bricks that built this house will be clay again and then a riverbed. Pay attention or you'll miss it. A gentle breeze follows every air raid but it does not know the blameless from the wicked. It simply swallows the whole town. I am a hostage. I live instead of some other matter and so I am more than the body I inhabit. I am enormous in my disappearing, bigger than the air that Texas is burning outside my window. Aban died without a whisper. The death of the other is the first death, mine follows his. That's how I killed him.

The future is ruined and encroaching on elections. Give bees the vote, is what everybody's thinking, or parrots. Bees smell the roses and never stake a claim, a parrot will tell you what is said behind closed doors. Rats spread disease. Aban used to walk all over town with his young son, when the boy wasn't sleeping he was talking, he explained. Everyone here has lost someone, and then everything else goes missing. Replaced by all things Asian via Houston, but the locals can't pronounce it. Gone too are the familiar smells from the evening meal, save a little parsley and raw onion on your breath. There is plenty of fuel in the ground and in tankers on their way to everywhere, but not a drop to cook with. Still, we should be grateful because so many Texas targets don't exist.

Enter the Texas messengers, what did the guard want … he's not a guard … can we turn him … what do you mean … to our side … what side is he on now … the other side … the other side of this side … I think so … you want him to turn … yes … to the other side … to this side … the side he's on … the other side … I don't understand … does he speak English … he's learning … what were you talking about … to be … to be what … the verb, I am, you are, he is … I am what … you just are … what … not what, are … are what … we haven't gotten that far yet … I just am then … you aren't really … what do you mean … you're not here … your point … I don't know … keep him talking … sure.

The measure of wealth is money my father said to me, and then he went on dying. He liked his fish deep-fried and battered, my mother prepared various kinds of sauces. I was born against my will and then surrendered to the interruption. Every day I work to find my anonymity but the lenses to see it have not been invented. My name is breaking my back. Bring me the clothes that will undress me, find me in a riddle. Mother I'm fine, every day Hakim brings me soup. Father, it's ok to buy your suits off the rack. I am speaking to you from the other side of the empire. I never liked either of you, and all of mankind. I promise not to move a muscle after I'm dead.

In the distance I could hear an Uzbek flute and a Palestinian oud. Each morning I put my ear to the floor to mark where the night has been. I see black spools and a crimson tongue scuttling underneath the furniture. In New York I pulled up roots, fastened my fingers to the wind and set out to find the infinite. It was in the kitchen. I will always have been mad. This lack is what in me has triumphed. I am not the weaver, but the weave and what believers cannot penetrate. Thank God I'm a sinner. War is when the righteous rally behind the king and revolution is when they agree to topple him. I do not ask what it means and we all know what happens next. They will surely hurt someone.

27

CNN IS REPORTING THAT I am not, not here, not there, not anywhere. It seems the bird is making good his refusal to disclose my whereabouts. He will be responsible for how this story ends, but there's no point brooding on what separates us. On this we agree. Your death will be as though a wedding feast, he said, so say the nuns in Boston. I asked if that was his experience as his carcass slowly faded just outside my window. He said the rules don't apply to him. In this room I have one care only, to peel a few more layers from my cranium. Each day I pray the waiting lengthens. Man dies, so there's no need for eternity. How thin, how trite God's promise, how meagre His rejoicing. I'll decide the parting that's in store for me. A rope, or a scene from Icarus perhaps, the final trajectory. I need something more than an acquittal.

In Nanking I watched them empty the river with a cup, pull the bodies one by one. It was 1937 and the crickets refused to sing, there was a smell of burning in the air. I arrived with a mouthful of promises from the President. The Japanese had come and gone. A man sitting by the river, a wanderer perhaps, watched as I stood frozen on the banks. It's ok to cry, he said, but don't drink the water. He played a small wooden xylophone with tiny mallets, the tips tightly wrapped in cotton fabric. He was accompanied by the rain that was falling on tin roofs. It's simple, he said when he saw I had a mind to listen, the difference between the dead and the living is, some are like this and some are like that. I left immediately. To the President I reported that we had much to learn from the Japanese.

The Texas messengers are serious about their work. Well ... well what ... your report ... on Tuesday I walked in the courtyard ... are you sure it was Tuesday ... no ... what else ... they're not going to kill me yet ... why not ... I'm on television ... what about the bird ... he flies back and forth from Berlin ... on what airline ... he's a bird ... and the mouse ... he is busy with the reconstruction … does he have a contract … I don't know … how often does he visit … he lives here … where are his things … things … tools, letters, pictures … he's not like us … oh … he's very philosophical … what does he say … freedom is a decision sustained by an infinite withdrawal as intensification of the nothingness, the founding gesture of non-being which does not know itself and is not free … he said that … I think so … how does he know … he studied in France.

It is difficult to gauge a well-satiated public, a groundless yawning swelling and diminishing. Hakim kneels to pray five times a day but, unlike his mat, the stones are unyielding. When we first met he asked if I was from New York … yes … you must know a lot of girls. It is dangerous to disrupt virtue, its will, to the contrary. Armies march in all directions, for every regiment a piper and so on to the king. At night I listen for my footsteps in the dark, the approach finally of what will not be said. It begins at birth and ends in the middle of a shipwreck. The talking part is in between. In the morning I see things differently, and that's the problem. Hakim is partial to things to which he can attach a number. He dreams of swarms armed and speaking with his tongue. Only what stands can fall, he says, and then it will be our turn. He longs for a fool's paradise, and killing.

Our President is a simple man with a direct line to heaven. Heaven is not a resting place. He is the prayer, the script domestic that breaks the rumour of unspeaking speech. He is the golden age of imperious repetition. He will bleed the Russians again and when necessary. These are not simple things. To stir assent with trinkets and command, real wages to build the machines of future battle. One villain after another will compel us beyond our final hour. Together we will march to kill the monster. The constant rumour of enchanted slaughter, always to come. Threats against the Gipper, narrow escape from Libyan hit men. Clear and cowboy strength to charm irreverent intellectuals, in Poland they were simply bulldozed into pits.

Restraint is a questionable word. Genghis Khan killed half and fed the rest, everyone longed for the latter. Then the other. A people will come full circle but the torture must go on, as in a love song, the baying and the madness. Close the border and release a winter's silence, people starving waiting to be killed. Eight hundred years later, during excavations in Mongolia, experts confirmed the legend but they could not separate the hero from his victims. Apparently we all look the same to an archaeologist. Empires fall to empires in waiting. Armies galloping across frozen plains and eventually, the silhouette of a tank as it slowly turns a corner. How threadbare is the future, people scuttling to find their place in the next millennium.

The town of Halabja is in Iraq, from Florida veer right at Virginia and head east. On March 21, 1986 Texas refused to sign a Security Council statement condemning Iraq's use of chemical weapons. In May of the same year the Department of Commerce licensed seventy biological exports to that country from anywhere but here. These included 21 batches of anthrax. In Texas no one could find Iraq on a map and the lead story is always in retail. Texas attacks in anticipation of the future. Beyond the noise, blood and filth there is no explanation. In 1988, Iraq attacked the Kurdish population in Halabja. I was part of a Texas delegation to replace the contaminated food. Our generosity speaks directly to the victim of our understanding, and to the meaning that eludes him up to and including the instant of his death.

We are winning and on the side of angels but be careful out there. Better yet, don't go anywhere. War is best served cold on every channel, without mornings, without sunsets. No one will argue with the ratings. The people will float in and out during commercials, or use the remote to attenuate the circumstances. Don't despair, a war is as good as a sandwich. The violence will go on and no one is responsible. Our crimes must exceed those charged to our enemies. We absolve our own and a small gallery of friends. Babydocmarcoshusseinseko of Zaire who fade to new favourites in the moment that we kill them.

Death and birth are the same word but for the time in between. This is obvious and in no way helpful but repeating it keeps us from disappearing. We never emerge in the life that is our own, it is the flight of a blind owl and a blind owl has a dim view of its community. Cut to the brain or is this the story, a fugitive frenzy, a complaint from the wrong side of the mirror. There must be a better way to forget what I'm saying. Texas is rising but its reign will not outlast a clock tower in Zurich or Geneva. Perhaps I should switch empires. If I ever get out of here I'll cross the line but first I'll have to find it. In 2003 we were at a crossroads, fix the President's grammar or invade Iraq. The former, it seems, was just too difficult and every country needs its heroes.

When next the levies break FEMA will supply the patio furniture and KFC has agreed to extend delivery service to the roof. Once we were fish, then beached and baking on a rock. That's when the trouble started. We adapted, some say, to a deeper wish and perhaps it's true. Fish still can't carry a tune. In New Orleans death is the pause in the pounding of a boogie-woogie beat that goes on and on until it disappears in the gap between two stars. An inch, approximately, between your thumb and forefinger. Less if a hurricane knocks out the power grid. Or you're face up in the Gulf of Mexico and you have to choose between your neighbour and your saxophone. So it goes. If you've seen one star you've seen two but you have to keep showing up because they won't shine without you.

Words get in through my ears, it doesn't matter if they're true. Eyes are the intermediary of the mind and the other way around. It takes all three to name a flower but any sound will do. Full stop. The pen waits for the hand to cease, it thinks it will do better on its own. In Manhattan I bought a gun. I kept it in my coat with six bullets in the chamber. In Central Park I talked to dogs and met with serious journalists. I showed them how to tiptoe through the horseshit, how to kill a little time. When I begin to count I'll count them in. I move from the table to Japan and back again, from this room I can go anywhere. If not for my visitors I would stay away for several years. The distance is the same exactly and, as any dog will tell you, one day equals seven.

I keep a running tally, a proper sum of what I know in the shoebox underneath my bed. For all the things that I don't know I'll need a bigger box, and a bigger audience. Hakim says the unknown won't fit inside my room but it's already here. I hold this truth to be self-evident and every night I rearrange it, to match the statistics. Experts will decide the body count and Wall Street needs a variant. In the morning I check the shoebox for a list of my utensils – one plate, one fork, one spoon and then I pair it with the inventory. I empty my chamber pot into the makeshift drain that runs through the courtyard to the vines. To my surprise they seem to do just fine. Hakim said they are also nourished by the bodies of the prisoners before me. In the ground I won't hanker for a following. There, he said, I can finally do some good.

28

As a diplomat I examined my ideas before they came to me, posed the problem of communication and crawled inside the explanation. I am the violence that I speak of but I leave the killing to the grownups, the mechanic and the butcher. In Calabria my grandfather knew how to be poor without irritating the rich and he didn't blame the state when a tooth fell out for good. When the day came he put on his jacket and reported to the post office. A bride is a wife and then a widow, her brother will kill the pig come January. That night thousands of men slept in trenches and sergeants all over Europe made it clear to each and every one, the alternative was worse. My grandfather was known by his middle name because he didn't have one. He wanted someone else to die.

You can be whatever you want in Texas, an apt resemblance of a rigorous contradiction, a beginning that coincides with the remains, an endless back to concrete emptiness, the assertion of a universal negation, a philosophy of the face, noise, a work of falling commentary, the truth about disagreement. During the Balkan wars Texas sold arms to the Croats with the help of Hezbollah. We also sold weapons to Israel, Greece and the Ukraine, who in turn sold them to the Serbs. Texas is this incessant vanishing and lays claim to every unknown soldier that can still shoot a rifle. In 1980 the cola wars went global and we finally understood that monuments are important, but a logo is worth dying for.

There is no freedom without death and Hakim said mine will be videotaped. I will play the part of a dead man, refute the soul's assertion and posit blindness as absolute unity. Then my character will disappear inside the work of the executioner. Hakim's video will break the secret, tell everyone where I've been. When the President sees it he will rekindle the nation's patriotism and Congress will loosen the purse strings. In this country no one will notice a few more thousand tons of ordinance. I have explained to Hakim that I have worked in

Hollywood and can be of more use behind the camera. That's my job, he said, but don't despair, there are no cheap seats to an assassination. I believe him but I can contribute so much to the more technical side of the enterprise.

My death is not the man I was. Discourage noble feelings in the young, they will be with me soon enough. Silence all battle cries, level the monuments and plant potatoes in the cemetery. Tell them we died in mud, blood and piss, and eternity was trampled by an elephant. I am running faster than my disappearing, trapped in the speed of my falling. My anguish is resolved in the death of each instant, as it succumbs to the next. Without me. These are the sounds the moment makes. A diamond is a grain of sand cut from eternity and fashioned round your throat to bend the light. Death to Darfur. At the end of my mind there is freefall through precious fear. I fucked it in the ear, took it up the ass and injected it into my veins. Still it is mute.

Let us not forget the violence we do unto others and in this hell have air to breathe. Let us seize what we already have. I will drop this marionette in the town square, reinvent the old rules under threat of a new failure. Let us agree that the new never arrives, he who enjoys art is a philistine and life is no longer. The President doesn't know how many wars it will take to win the peace. Scholars will debate the words and annotate the injured tenses. New England poets will hurl precisely fired Bostonian bricks, wine-stained, thinner than blood. Analysis to follow. One day the President turned and whispered awkwardly in my ear. I was wondering if you knew, he asked, why my head so frequently detaches from my body and why the people hate me.

One morning I decided to move ahead my weeping. I thought this reminiscing of things to come would help me to discard old habits. Admittedly this is a loose calculation. A body soon to be stemmed is not likely to change. It remains what it is for what little is left. I am no longer needed in the castle and I have forgotten the taste of apples. This room is my home now, my America. I studied all the maps long before I approached the border and yet no one here agrees with my geography. I pace the length and width, search for the hands that laid the stones that fix my step, the hands that hoisted the beam from which I will hang myself. Surely they have left me a note that will deliver me weightless, winged perhaps.

When the curtain fell on the Second World War the English went again to find the countryside, a patch of green and the butterflies in Northern Ireland. In 1952 Stalin suggested that Germany could be reunited on the condition that it not join any military alliance against the Soviet Union. Which seemed reasonable since every couple of decades Germany set themselves to killing Russians. The only thing worse than death is a statistic, Stalin explained. For Eisenhower the situation was more complicated. He gave speech after speech with precisely the right number of commas but he never said anything about the Russian proposal to reunite the Rhineland. Instead he rearmed West Germany, launched the space race and expanded the biggest military industrial complex since the beginning of the world. The Russians, he said, are not like us.

Soon we were in Vietnam or at least that's how I remember it. The official target within a free bombing zone is anything that moves. It's been thirty-five years but the day we went in is still classified. Perhaps it was a Monday and Tuesday never came. That war was not a tragedy because in a tragedy the hero has to die. According to Arthur Schlesinger, special assistant to President Kennedy for Latin American affairs and Harvard professor, the bombing of Vietnam was the most accurate and restrained in the history of warfare and an expression of our goodwill. A subtlety lost on two million children, give or take five million, born with deformities from thirty million, give or take forty million, gallons of herbicide and agent orange. Mute is the language we're looking for, the clarity you came in with. Everything disappears – houses, crops and the light in Asia.

Hope is a retreating army, a bullet waits for a head to jerk upright and then there's no hurry. I'm in this room because I was arrested for espionage, or war crimes. These are not things for me to decide. I will not be attending my own execution. I'll watch it from a terrace in France perhaps, where it's good to be alive. Or Italy, there it's an art to forget your appointments. In the 1960s everyone was in the middle of a long life. The young thought we may not have to litter the planet with body parts. When the decade ended everybody went home. Dying is something to do while you wait in your room. Texas is building a mirror in the sky. It will shoot laser beams, just like in *Star Wars*. The shield and the spear to strike anyone, anywhere, anytime, subject to the normal accidents of such a complex system.

During the Spanish Civil War, Texaco sold oil to Franco. It was widely reported in Europe and Latin America but the *New York Times* just couldn't break the story. Texas will tolerate a democracy but it prefers a dictator and a measure of squalor. A nod and plenty of money to him who controls the army. If that's not enough we'll throw in a visit to the biggest nipple in Washington. We'll run the numbers for the sake of our shareholders, expose the bounty, they must not be denied. Nothing beats math to appropriate the scraps, elections will help identify the opposition. We'll need at least one generation on the verge of starvation, hereafter referred to as labour. The courts will allocate time to the naysayers, and the banks will still take deposits.

In the summer everybody leaves the city, backpacks and hiking shoes, the human tribe on a pilgrimage to the interior. Which turns out to be a fish, recently tossed, dazed with one eye up on the bed of your canoe. It doesn't know what hit him and you won't either. In the south of Spain they leave town in the winter, abandon their saints and hand the keys to the British. The Empire isn't what it used to be, but a commoner can still afford a rented Christmas in the pubs of Andalusia. They look exactly like the pubs in Stratford. The descendants of many a revolution have had to pick themselves up, dust themselves off, and sling beer for the English. Picasso preferred a kiss to silence and silence to a word, give me oils, he said, and I'll paint you a war. *Guernica* is how the people got even.

The country where I am held prisoner is no longer friendly, and everyone weeps behind locked doors. Hakim has asked me to stop pretending. The editor too, said I should just tell the story, name names and then she'll get me to a book signing. I'm trying but I was never here, and I took these words from a dying man's ear. Further, it was much easier to tell a school from a parking lot when this place was still a republic. Without the roof the classrooms seem much less crowded and in place of a bell there's a siren. The teachers will tell you the children are learning much more now, more than they ever will from the book I'm writing. Geography, for example, is no longer about rivers, mountains and plains. It's their destiny, the luck of the draw, and there's no way to assign a grade to their progress.

In 1965 I gave Suharto a list on behalf of the CIA. It was compiled over decades by our missionaries doing God's work in villages all over Indonesia. I updated the list as people were killed or imprisoned. Ten years later I provided him a similar list for the invasion of East Timor. It got less attention because the population of that country was only six hundred thousand. Some of them were communists. Gerald Ford blessed the mission and wished Suharto Godspeed. It seems the island state was planning an assault against the one hundred and forty million people of Indonesia. One third of the population on the island was slaughtered, East Timor is now less of a threat. We're keeping our eye on the rest.

29

Whenever possible I turned with my son toward the nearest mountain. We camped by a slow-moving creek. So many things delighted him, wild rabbits, maps and strawberry jam. His gaze uncluttered by the killing kings. For all of August he slept hand in hand with a squirrel. I didn't know that on its own the air could be so simple. Your life is still to come, I said, but for the moment let's assume that we are here. After so many words we'll stop and think things over, rephrase the question so the answer never comes. Father, already there is discipline growing all over my body. Look how playful the sun is, peeking in and out of these darkened canyons that trap and split the wind. It is not for us to tear them down again, light a fire and get us through this night.

In September we climbed down the mountain on steps of braided smoke. I went first, to catch him should he fall. I took great care not to speak too soon or return his look. What I realized sitting by that creek never made it to my brain, never made it to my throat. This was not the time for gossip or a rope, and nothing cuts like daddy's voice. All month long there had been a smell of burning in the air. New York was smouldering and heroes were emerging from under a crowd of corpses. I was hoping they would not kill us both. I told my son to keep his eyes and ears wide open. When he dies it will not be from a single gunshot or a falling tower. He will know to die of everything. My son, from this room I cannot say goodbye. Let's agree to meet in graveyards where we will always be together.

Aban is dead but he is not like the bird. He never visits. I can still hear his cackle and his ramble, his dog-eared verses. The day he died he asked me why I was so pale. I'm afraid, I said, Texas is what Texas does. Now I pace the length, width and the perimeter of a rectangle, approximately. The fireplace spans a corner and disrupts the symmetry from the floor to the ceiling. I stand on a chair to touch the timber, the rib that keeps everything from buckling. Engineers built this house and the Acropolis. Architects draw pictures. President Clinton understood the difference when he launched a cruise missile through the chimney of a pharmaceutical factory in Khartoum. Outstanding in its precision with minimal damage to the surrounding area. Except for the tens of thousands that died subsequently of malaria.

Vespucci was a pimp and of Columbus the natives asked the willow if they should let the stranger in. The willow didn't answer, that's how they knew to listen. In his log Columbus recorded hills that looked like women's breasts. History, he wrote, is the sound of my own voice. We are all Americans now. Explorers adorn the halls of power on canvas, stone or bronze. The names of airports are reserved for presidents, capacity will be matched to their popularity. The best measure of a leader is the body count but it isn't practical to record every shot, every missile, there's just no way to track it. A tally, one clean statistic will keep the victims from forever disappearing. The lessons of history will be easily remembered if to each administration we can attach a number.

One night God and I almost hammered out an agreement. In return I promised to relinquish what I planned to keep. So much for my ill-spent years, my happy sinning. He said I could keep the screaming, which is what I did each time our meetings ended. I'm old and it's late, he said, we'll pick this up again in the morning. In the morning He was nowhere to be found. I looked in the courtyard, in every kitchen cabinet and inside the fireplace. Everywhere I looked the mouse was looking back at me. What have you done with God, mouse … God is everywhere … is he under the bed … that's not everywhere. I crossed the room to study my face in the mirror. My reflection was agreeable of late and I was tired of the mouse's wit. It's good I won't be here, said the voice inside the glass, when you grow a double chin.

My mind is demanding retribution and to make matters worse, I'm being persecuted by the sun. I have told my captors all my secrets and if I am released I will immediately end this silly rhyming. You're centuries late, said the bird, and you have lousy timing. Texas is a rolling war, a catastrophe for the ages. It is its own impossibility. When the Spanish set sail for Mexico and Peru they brought smallpox. That's how they knew God was on their side. They held a king for ransom, a room full of Inca gold and two of silver. Then they killed him anyway. My body is where I wait to die, more or less. In Greenwich Village they would not paint my portrait. The artists were conflicted, à la carte or the tasting menu. I am who I was, but this time I will refuse.

Texas knows what there is to know about oil, cows and your postal district. It took a lot of plainclothesmen to put that sentence together. I was born hapless as a bird, free as a beggar. First I was betrayed and then I learned to plunder or the other way around. I gave everything to the Pentagon but they were not impressed. I am a man already dead but for a single blow. In Berlin I wore a trench coat and talked mostly from the corner of my mouth. My job was to protect the free world but I cannot waste a minute more to calm the living. The display windows in Manhattan feed a billion Asians, backs bent, fingers bleeding. China rising. I'm just looking for a place to turn, a place to end. A glance, an ache before I make another sound.

Tell me again, Texas, how the enemy in Chile was embedded in the eye of his neighbour and why so many went missing between the kitchen and their front door. I am not one to leave things hanging and from this room I can still get things done. I washed the blood from the steps but it did nothing to stem the pain. The dead are tired of our lies, they can no longer remain silent. Mr. President, it seems we are not done with that hemisphere. Remember if you close an eye you can block the sun with just your thumb. Mothers in Chile have only one photo and it's pinned directly to their chest. Two heads are better than one and it is heartening to see them spend time with their sons. They are old, still a threat, but pictures fade. They too will disappear on the streets of Santiago.

Mr. President I regret that I will not be attending any more meetings. I have run out of ideas but I will be available for the things that don't matter. I still dress myself but only in the dark, to avoid the arguments I have with my shadow. He is a stickler for the uniform and a menace with a light bulb. There is also the issue of who's dressing whom. Murder has crossed my mind but Hakim digs only one grave per prisoner. Eternity, it seems, dictates a reckoning. I am not at all certain I'll be here tomorrow, and so yesterday I recited all I know to Rimbaud. His ears were still tingling from the old books. He wrote down everything I said and never wrote another word. Then he drowned himself in Africa. He was a kid, molten and still grieving from the bottom of some nameless river. He died waiting for your call.

The day that I was captured was like any other. The city was at a standstill except for the army. People waited in endless lines to put gas in their cars, but the Middle East, it seems, had run out of fuel. Aban and I were in the small office next to the marketplace with a canvas bag full of money. Aban concerned himself with its dispersal and watched as I took notes. This is not real money, he said … really ... it's obvious ... oh ... look at it ... it looks real … exactly … I don't understand … the real money doesn't exist. Then a young man walked into the courtyard and shot him. The assassin must have known about the money because he just left it there. They took me instead. I would have preferred a death on the Hudson, last words from a bridge to a few puzzled cats and a duck.

Early in the seventeenth century I was in Spain. I logged incoming treasure and reviewed contracts for a commission. The gold was shipped out the day it came in. The king was busy crushing infidels in France, Turkey, Portugal, Italy and some other places. The treasure went north to London and weapons south to Madrid. By mid century the Spanish king was broke and no longer in need of a middleman. That's how the Spanish built the British Empire. I followed the money. The English king decided to sit on the gold so I went back to Virginia to help Jackson with his Indian problem. I wrote treaty after treaty to protect the new homeland from the indigenous population. A people will consent to deception if it delays annihilation.

I was raised on chestnuts and mushrooms, one dead pig in January and a few potatoes between wars. Sleep is hard to come by and the lack of it distorts everything, but the years have not been terrible. These wounds are someone else's, a stranger without wings. Heads will roll, he says, and then rattles the keys to my prison room. I had a job – lie, but I kept a list of what I said and a map of where I'd been. With Jesus I built castles in the sand. When they pulled him down I followed the procession to the tomb. Fuck the Promised Land, he said, I'm going to Texas. I winked and said I'll see you there. As for the thieves, one repented and the other said Jesus, get us out of here. For them there was no stone casket, and the earth was nailed directly to their foreheads.

30

Last night I was in the Bronx, a poker game flashing jacks and queens. I drank, lost and drank some more. The bird sat in the chair opposite. Your strategy, he said, is too transparent ... there's plenty I'm not saying, bird, don't assume I'm a victim to this telling. Then he took all the money I had and didn't have. It's all over, he said, but for the crying and the laughing ... it ends when I say it ends, and if I were you I wouldn't get too close to my shoe. When I drink I can be quite belligerent. The next day I pulled myself together and noticed I was not hungover. That's how I knew it was a dream. I decided not to tell the bird, nothing good would come of it. I'm going back tonight to pay my debt and suggest we make the game a regular event. If one day I don't show up there will be questions.

Old men long absent from the hills of Naples or Kirkuk visit me in this room, or perhaps I call them and they come. We sit and talk awhile, they do not wish me harm. I could draw them with a pickaxe or a gun. Only the dead can explain why we are so happy and so frightened. I prefer my new companions to the ones still kicking. Amongst the living change is not permitted. What was it like, I ask … I took a wife and sold figs to the English ... how did that work out ... some of my children survived ... I see ... but I never visited the Grand Canyon ... oh ... or learned to play the piano ... I'm sorry ... would you like to know about heaven ... no ... it's far ... that makes sense ... anything else before I go ... how do I dispose of a dead bird ... get a cat.

In Greece I backed the fascists. France protected Algeria from the Algerians, Haiti from the Haitians. Prime Minister Lester Pearson of the north railed against the Russians in Vietnam, wherever there were none, amidst Texans by the thousands cancelling elections in plain view. They gave him the Nobel Prize and an airport in Toronto. 1962 was a good year for Dow Chemical, a mountain of new bones. Did I mention Ethiopia, Mussolini's plan, thick like Ezra Pound, like his six hundred pigs in a basement. Everywhere we regret the fatherland, and what should never have been said. A bird is not a bird and a pipe is not a pipe. Things of the imagination never hit their mark.

In Texas, God doles out the souls and he favours gated neighbourhoods. He sees the beauty inside all of us but that's no way to assign an address. The biggest clan lives behind the Great Wall of China but our Lord won't consort with communists. Archaeologists have traced all this back to our tangled roots and their work is not subject to the vagaries of metaphor. The arranging of stones will outlast a poem, and where the ancients built their borders the experts will confirm a massacre. All findings point to death. The analysts are working their way through the centuries and every year the science just gets better. It's gaining on forever. In 1869 they will invent barbed wire.

In the first half of the last century old man Kennedy allegedly sailed ships under cover of night. Oak barrels in rough waters, luckily the trip was a short one, from Cuba to a few Miami warehouses or across Lake Ontario. It was the roaring twenties and Camelot was just a shit-house in the yard. Many historians don't believe this story but no one disputes his insider trading. Let's be clear, Joseph Kennedy was not some syphilitic gangster. It takes a certain etiquette to keep up with the Rockefellers, it takes money to win the White House. After 1959 Joe never went back to the island, and Castro sold his sugar to the other superpower. Havana moved to Nevada and the son pardoned the father. It was peace President Kennedy wanted, according to the evidence produced after his death, a record so secret it will never be found. There just wasn't time to fix poppy's alibi.

In 1963 the Kennedy administration backed a Baathist coup against the Iraqi government. They wanted to help rid the country of suspected communists. They had grown to one half of one percent of the population. Mobil, Bechtel and British Petroleum had to be protected. Saddam at the time was a very young man and the Baath Party secretary. A peach, waiting to ripen so he could do grownup things like mimic a deity. Saddam helped the CIA compile lists of educated Iraqis, some only he could identify. Then he offered to kill them. I was sent with a suitcase filled to bursting, the same age-old diplomacy. I paid informers and kept the President current, complicit in the death and torture of several thousand Iraqi citizens. Then as now the coup went fine but the peace was a bitch. At least the Baath Party knew not to fire the army and the constabulary.

Grain is for eating but first creditors must be paid. At sundown we dance and burn Hebrews. Nobles wear a mask. History fills many volumes but it has only one subject, we came and then we could not flee. Our stay is but a few blue mornings. I can tell by what is said at closing time, of what in all of this is real. As for the angels, they have already been invented. Praise Texas from every soup kitchen and steeple, from every satellite in heaven. Its stupidity must not go unheeded. For Caesar I worked a chisel, for Napoleon a quill, but this time I am afraid. Everyone is moving in the same direction. I set out from the inside of my head, arrived here and there, cancelling one step at a time.

During the silk wars I was drunk and in the street, the stench of flesh in my mouth. It was fine. These hills were cut by generations of slaves with a Roman blueprint. A sardine is bought at one price and sold for another, that's all you will ever need to know. Kissinger mused on the problem of history, everyone hates me, he thought, because I am so good. He couldn't understand why those who could not stop the bombs from falling refused to negotiate. History is made, he told the President. Flaming cartwheels running naked in the jungle, in and out and disappearing, in the same instant. Embryos floating in a blue lake of dead water. Foliage cleared to the bedrock, lets the sunshine, the sunshine in.

In 1989 we ended the Cold War but the mouse doesn't seem to know that. History is how we decide who owns what, truth imitates thinking. There will be time for both in eternity but in this world, said the mouse, it's the cheese I'm after. All that's left to do is decide a lifetime of furniture and negotiate hard for every grain of sand. This country underestimated our commitment to its liberation, but if it only produced cucumbers many of its people would still be alive. In Texas repetition is our crystal ball. One massacre and then another with a decade or so in between. Tomorrow I will have to live again but there's nothing I want. At the instant of my death I will still be waiting. Words are my eyes, bubbles and puddles, crates.

Stop taking notes, said the mouse ... why ... it distracts from the conversation ... I have to record all coming and going ... really ... apparently ... that's odd ... and everything we say ... why ... reporting purposes ... who do you report to ... the Texas messengers ... do they exist ... I'm not sure ... who else ... the bird ... the bird doesn't exist ... I know ... that's a problem ... what is ... no one is reading your reports ... what difference does that make ... confirmation ... of what ... that they exist ... that's why I take notes ... what do you mean ... so I'll be ready ... for what ... to report ... perhaps you should report to me ... do you exist ... of course I exist ... as a mouse ... precisely ... with perfect syntax ... well ... how do you explain that ... I studied in Berlin ... I thought that was the bird ... are you sure ... I think so ... check your notes.

I could get out of this place if I could just fix the alphabet. The first thing I would do is write a letter to Congress comprised only of vowels, introduce the hard consonants after they'd mastered the howling. Just the chorus this time, a tragedy without the corpses. Yesterday I sent a memo to Texas via the messengers, then I pleaded with the bird to release my coordinates … I can't … why not … I'm a bird … will you teach me to fly … no … why not … you don't have a passport ... the mouse thinks you don't exist ... I'm here aren't I ... that's true ... let me see your report ... this is my report ... anything else ... the mouse says I should report to him ... does he exist ... he says he does ... decide and let me know.

In Calabria I went looking for a bridge that spanned two rivers. The sign at the airport said this way to your dead grandfather. There must have been fewer buildings when last he was here. Some were bombed and later replaced, others were new and some I have invented. Suffice to say everything had increased. When I saw my grandfather I said nothing of the changes. He spoke to me of things half imagined, empty words, confused and identical to my own. He told me of a pink-purple flower in the mountains of Oregon whose aboriginal name has been lost forever. Those hills are remote, he explained, and filled with death, but the black bear and the cougar are not disturbed. They do not have a word for it. Dying is easy and not very important, he said, but we must find that flower.

The Texas messengers are back. We'd like to set up a meeting with the bird and the mouse … at the same time … preferably … they don't get along … why not … one is a bird the other a mouse … one at a time then … the bird then the mouse … the order is not important … it's so hard to plan … you will introduce us … inevitably, what should I tell them … we need them to play a more decisive role in bringing democracy to the region … like in El Salvador … yes, but with more enthusiasm … I'll go tell the bird … where is he … Berlin … you can wait till he returns … are you sure … yes … what is to become of me … you will be killed … is that necessary … we can use it to rally morale and we don't know where you are … the bird knows … he can't tell us … why not …. he's a bird … have you any suggestions … hang on to your delusions.

In El Salvador I suggested sequential, identifiable ballots in clear plastic boxes to secure an orderly election. Then I posted monitors at every polling station and told them to put on their sunglasses, mirrored, standard issue. Their orders were to maintain reading distance. I was hoping for a real death, muzzled and light as a cork. Not this brooding carcass lashing against all tides. Let me go empty as I began, enough seen, enough said. Texas steers rainbows into mountains and kills those who disagree. It can dial up your mother faster than your aunt and watch her pick up the phone from any one of a thousand space satellites. I showed you pictures of the two of them talking. That's how you knew I was on your side.

In Babi Yar I watched them jump like maddened cattle. The rain in Kiev is the same as the rain in Texas and though I cannot say for sure that I was there, nor name the century, it is not important. Things are no different now. I gather the dates that are in this room. From my window I see Gaza and the Sudan. I see the Brooklyn Bridge. My ears are bleeding from the burst that delivered a child's ribbon to the wind. It's gone. We are the dead. We are loaded into trains, beaten and then machine-gunned on the edge of canyons. We are drowned, gassed and burned into matter, into numbers. Heaven is charged with our disposal, all the while speaking of other things. We are adrift, not dead – death.

Texas no longer sends praise so I no longer know what to do, and oaths come and go. The deaths I commissioned were for the common good. Once upon a time Jesus walked the earth, later someone invented the double bass. In 1917 the British took Baghdad, they said they would be leaving soon. In 1975 I reported to Wolfowitz. One morning I told him the Chinese were afraid of a Soviet attack. We should increase weapons sales to the region, especially to Taiwan. I was right. That year Wolfowitz and I played golf. He was promoted and so was I, to his assistant. In 1986 he took me to Indonesia. Suharto, he said, is our kind of guy. My job was to agree with him. Before we left I treated myself to a haircut and a sandwich. One should not assume an interest in history from the things I'm saying. It only takes a minute to get the body count.

31

THE STORY. THERE WAS a woman, a wounded space. I could not agree to a reduction of my own peril. We reached to stop, to hide in quick frightened glances lost in the habit of consecutive time, apparently without end. We lived on the precipice that is departure, arrival again and again for which we were not present. Together we forgot talk, to remember, kept going, in the dark I mean, awash in the pain of not touching and touching all. We did not despair, we didn't know how but we knew what to imitate. The disaster is not where we plunder and it's not in this room. It's in a café on Broadway, but it would be better if there were no one to tell these stories to.

The story before. My wife is a lawyer, a doctor in Africa. I met her in Paris at a forum in Latin America. A powerful paper on monetary policy or infectious diseases, she is an expert you see. We had a child in New York, Texas, a brownstone and a Volkswagen, very chic and within walking distance. The café on the corner was where we read books on war and poetry. We objected to violent abduction in the night, which always took place after taking place. We were uninterrupted in the past. In New Orleans they are rebuilding the sky without me. I had a job, I went every day. Weekends I spent with the wife and kid whom I adore, I adore, whom I adore. Then we talked about talking somewhat on the subject of these unions, agreement on ground about ground apportioned.

The story, again. On Wall Street I bought and sold numbers against the clock, sold my fortune for a fortune. The state agreed to lose my name and I began again as my reflection. In shop windows I noticed that I only cried at night and in the rain. The result is striking, said the woman who would marry me, but I have never understood the things you say. Go and look up your old address, she said, find out where your father bought his cigarettes. Concern yourself with complaints as they are practiced here. That's the thread we're hanging from.

Let us go then you and I, and choose our appliances. That's the night I found her and the night that she left me, the night we started building our betrayal.

The end. At first light I came to your bed. I told you about a talking mouse and a dead bird that would visit me in a room where I had not yet been. It would be best if we never went out, I explained. Like every other morning you dressed and walked out the door. I slept through your day. That night you came home shivering and asked for nothing, nothing from this world. In the morning you changed your mind, walked me to the door and handed me a lunch-bucket. There are women who live inside a drop of water, I protested. Small cuts each day, you said, is how we pay the rent, no one notices. I promised then I would learn the future, that in you my work would grow small. I set sail for the seventeenth century, Salem, Massachusetts to make my fortune. I sold names to the bishop. The mouse has assured me that my work will go on. Honey, I think we made the right decision.

One night I fashioned a cross from sticks and string, knelt by the fireplace. The bird thought this unreasonable, yours is to persist, is that so difficult … I am weak … strength has nothing to do with it … the Texas messengers want to meet with you and the mouse … at the same time … preferably … never … one at a time then … what have you told them … that I feel better when I am standing on my head … why would that interest them … they're ok with it … what else have you told them … everything … from now on you report only to me … you're a bird … your point … I'm not sure ... when are they coming back ... who ... the messengers ... they didn't say ... record their visits, see if there's a pattern ... what should I tell them about the meeting … stall … how … tell them I am still in Berlin.

In the time of time past my grandfather walked for five hours, more or less, fifteen thousand steps to a bridge where two rivers meet. He jumped. There are details that should not be overlooked and they will not be given. The bridge is not very high, I suspect he drowned. He went in search of a word that leaves no mark and gathers in the places it has never been, a word he could kill. *He*, is that word. It lives in the never, and that night he, or it, slipped into the river. In the interest of history the telephone had not yet been invented or there was not one around. The mail was delivered monthly. The city now has an airport and a train will take you downtown. The bridge is still there and within hollering distance of the river below.

I am the last-born of a peasant father. Chestnut strings were drying next to a basement fire, mushrooms waited to be gathered in the pines. After the war, chestnuts and mushrooms kept us alive. Before that we simply starved. The men were stationed by the sea to ward off the invasion. On the beach you won't need boots, said the captain. He still had his. Then he ordered everyone to just keep on winning. Autumn clouds turn the town a deeper grey and old soldiers are walking their memories. They are nostalgic for the things they can no longer do, or do to you. I come here to find the price of my leaving. Everyone is looking for the same thing, death and a story. This is neither. Humour me until it's over.

Her eyes were grey and sometimes blue. I could not find her among the traffic lights that dot the city. They had not seen her in the café where they know my name. There was a time for understanding, because I could not have her. I tell my story to the bird. He says everyone has betrayed me and he will too. Trust and betrayal are two ends of a pendulum, he explains, a wrecking ball for every house on the street. When the bird goes I will review my notes, decide where I've been and plan my next trip. Then I'll come back and report everything, the crossing and the stumbling. If he believes the things I say I'll change the story. I remember when we sank ships and played music all through the night, the dead drifting, glistening by the light of the moon.

I am learning a housefly's technique, trapped between two panes and before it settles for its last nap on the windowsill. The air is all outside. I am where the heart still beats and I'm fine with a noun but I have trouble with tenses, and walls. *'I was'* are words with which to pass into the day without god. I was in Cosenza when they pulled me out of a river that pours into another beneath a bridge. I have replaced everything because everything is missing. I am writing in English, a distance separated by commas and an ocean that whispers of a stream where I am still weeping. Waiting to be born. Then this will end, better for having tried, or worse.

When I landed in Boston, chickens cost a dollar and a half.

We happened upon these shores, the discarded livestock of less able kings. Bled the foot to heal the crown, unlearned our vocables to keep faith with a New York bondsman. We hid the sun under riverbeds and quiet fields, set out to deliver the blood of others. It is best to bomb people when they are on the brink of starvation. Not many can say no to a war after decades of squalor. A job is a job, especially in Mississippi. We are stand-ins in a cowboy fiction, numbers to a White House contingency, a footnote in a Broadway production. We are amassing on the Mexican border, looking for a crack in the fence. For years we've been digging this tunnel, we're coming up through the floorboards. It's taking forever to get to this sentence. Then we are gathered, parboiled and sold as a ham salad.

Enter the mouse, where are your notes … here they are … what language is this … I don't know ... what do you mean ... I found it on the floor … I see … really … when will they attack … who … he pointed east, west, up and down, a downpour, he said … I don't understand … these are your words not mine … that's true … one eye and never the same face … and back again … without hope … is that bad … of course not … what are my instructions … the bird didn't tell you … he's studying in Berlin … oh yes … what are my instructions … about what … the war … which one … this one … which side are you on … our side ... the other side of their side … the other side of this side … I see ... really … shut up for a moment will you … is that possible … perhaps by chance … how would I know … what difference does that make … this and not that, perhaps … don't be ridiculous … first things first … impossible … one word would cease to follow the other … unlikely … the stutter before the notion … stop … I can't.

32

WHAT WAS AND WHAT will be is not quite, so it cannot be measured or duplicated. You can't see it from the bell tower in the paragraph that comes after this one, but I think it's north. Nowhere, with the red sunset. It's easier there for a secret to penetrate. Death, for example, is the same everywhere but in the north no one feels the need to improve on it. Besides, after a fresh snow it's impossible to say where you've been. What men know is if you're lucky enough to take a wife she will love you, and then she'll outlive you. In 1999 Harry Connick Jr. wrote a song about it called "Nowhere with Love" and it goes something like this, I really don't know much at all and if you think I'm simple you're on the ball but I'm going nowhere, nowhere with love. A song of course is meant to be heard and not read, from a stage or on a gramophone, but in the Arctic you can't buy a ticket, the inventory at the company store is quite limited.

In 1994 I was in Rwanda administering another Texas absence. It was a barren land of Hutus and Tutsis, but to a giraffe we all look the same. The people there still sleep in their clothes and seldom go out alone. *Did you wake* is how they say good morning. The witness must be blind to see if she is to provide us with consolation from that which she must free herself. Rape and an oncoming bulldozer is not much to look forward to. May her words ring from every bell tower (there it is), may they bring comfort to children born of violence and a pointless paternity. When next she addresses the United Nations she will learn that tea and coffee from Africa are all the rage in Brussels and in Berlin.

While I was there, in Rwanda that is, I shook hands with General Romeo Dallaire, who shook hands with the devil. Satan, he said, was a young man with an AK-47, or a machete. Behind his eyes, the general recalled, there was nothing. Romeo was a French Canadian, a peacekeeper from Ottawa, he pleaded with me to take his story back to the President. If you ever get out of here move to New York, I suggested, the Queen rarely visits, and thanks to Woody Allen, everybody knows we have better therapists. A swift death is the last hope of a body soon to be stemmed. A debt paid to him who wields an end to the light, that he might turn quickly to some other matter. Dear God, let the merrymaking begin but first kill us, we can be of more use after the massacre. Hollywood will seize an opportunity and, unlike General Dallaire, Nick Nolte will rally the international community.

Cut to Pauline in Butare, portly and colourful in her wrap and spectacles, we see her on the back of a jeep with a bullhorn. She is the town's favourite daughter and the Rwandan minister of family and women's affairs. The Red Cross has arrived, there's food and sanctuary in the stadium. Her voice is too large for her body. Pan to thousands of Tutsis as they gather in the playing field and lower bleachers. The director is frustrated, it takes a lot of time and money to set up an hour of carnage, and he's worried it won't play in the Hamptons. Rape them before you kill them, we hear the voice again, they are not women they're cockroaches. But the soldiers had been killing all day and they were tired. Pauline stepped down from behind her bullhorn and unlocked the trunk to her jeep. Inside were several jerrycans filled with gasoline. Just burn them then, she said.

Hakim has brought my food and he is looking for conversation so let's begin. He says I don't have to worry about a Rwandan-style death. My executioner is skilled, and for him, death is an ordinary event. Do you mind if I eat while we talk, I'm very hungry ... please do ... with Jesus I crossed the then known world on a donkey ... did you ... and later I flew a rocket to the moon ... really ... then I rode the ass back to New York ... I see ... my neighbour, the actor from Montana, was waiting for me ... oh ... still in his underwear ... that's odd ... and a hat ... what did he say ... nothing, he just tipped his hat ... and you ... I thanked him for being there ... are you sure this happened ... no ... that's good ... but it's clear as lightning ... oh ... in a box ... I see ... transcendent ... sounds like it ... infinite ... apparently ... without all that wasted space.

Texas decides who lives and who goes to Vegas, that's because they understand us. After the printing press monks no longer had to transcribe books so they took to schooling young boys. Later we invented various recording devices and at CIA headquarters they have several decades on tape. Some say this loss of privacy is a blemish on the Constitution. The President swears it's to protect us from foreigners. I am in favour of premeditated madness, when I speak I know not to listen. So does Hakim. He's amused by my last-minute grasping. I think you're confused, he said ... confused, or am I absent ... absent ... and present ... let's change the subject. In Rwanda there were few places to hide and soon we received word from every town and pasture. Before mobilizing the hunters danced and sang songs. Finally the international community rushed to aid the victims, from the standpoint of those who were not there.

I could rebuild the earth if I could find the cliff from which I was hurled, but I'm having trouble locating the unthinkable. I am already of a certain age, well past my prime. I no longer speak to the young, unless it's to nourish their penchant for arson. If not you, who, I explain. Then I retire to invent my arrival. My departure will take care of itself. I hope I don't get them mixed up. I write it all down on scrap pieces of paper. I have ruined the beginning but I'm still working on the end. From time to time I stop to check the blood vessels pulsating out of my forehead. That's how I know I'm close to a breakthrough. I've been here for weeks now, or millennia. I can't tell from these markings. Be they on stone, bark or etched into the skin of an animal. Everything was here, or wrenched from the hands of a stranger.

I remember a Friday night in August, at least that's what it says on a ticket stub in the shoebox under my bed. I must have presented myself, the ticket snug in my pocket. This marvel of proof and belonging that is with me still. The self as a stand-in. I was one, the other and the adaptation. Death suspended for the sake of the show, an evening with my fellow man in the grotto. A movie on 42nd Street, an orgy of murder in English. I'm against it. I wept and then consoled myself with a hotdog, is how I like to tell it. That was my life in New

York. If I had more time I would begin at the beginning, like that book, *Earth*, by Jon Stewart. I don't dispute its importance but the real story ended with the first tracing, the instant we surrendered our grasp to a rock. What happened subsequent is merely conjecture.

When history broke with the past I moved to the country. I spent my days and nights on the veranda listening to the squeaky boards beneath my rocker. I kept a shotgun behind the front door. I had everything I needed and when God came to call I shot him, just like the rest of them. Then I buried him in a place that has never existed. Philosophy will play upon the strings of an invisible harp until it is blinded by our arrival. If I were a bird I would not state my country, I would sing in praise of space and days without names. I would make available my notes that prove nothing happened in the nineteenth century. Of the gentry, all can be glimpsed from their deeds of sale.

In Gaza only the birds come and go, they're on top of the paperwork but still susceptible to a wayward missile, or a bullet. The good news is there are almost no windows left to smash into, unlike the West Bank. All those new, four-level townhouses are a real menace. Elections are fine so long as they turn out the right way. The end is when all things will fit together again. God will forgive us our debts in this world and the next. Each time Sharon put Arafat in jail he asked, what do your people want. We want that which is no more. Here history is backdated by a rabbi and abbreviated to coincide with the building code. A permit is the same as a wink. Time is a wrecking ball, try to pack your things before lunch.

A catastrophe can always get worse and so never arrives. In New York we grazed on movies but occasionally we attended musicals in citadels with central heating. A swarm in evening dress behind glass and concrete. The women wore skins similar to their own but the animals didn't have their eye for fashion. The last production I saw was about the genocide in Darfur. The cast swallowed softly during the recitation while an orchestra mimicked screaming, loud at first and subsiding in the second act. This is the sound of a violence more common elsewhere. Atrocity is better suited to secondary markets, off Broadway essentially. I was there closing night, but I can't say for sure because I no longer have that ticket stub. After the show the actors went to a bar and the characters froze to death in midtown.

The sinking of the *Titanic* put an end to modernity. When they pulled in the bodies our romance with machines disappeared. People waited for days and then forever. I was there to take in the ocean. My plan was to write the book for pocket change and wait for the movie. I wore a top hat to protect my balding head and, given time, I would fix the economy. On arrival I took a look around, stepped quietly over the corpses and left immediately. Smoke was rising from chimneys nestled in foothills from where a stone path beckoned, well worn to the interior. I put one foot in front of the other and climbed a mountain to the sun. It was easy, but first I had to refute the story I'm telling. Apparently it's too much and too little. A few syllables short, said the bird, if you catch my meaning.

33

In 1962 I was dispatched to Vietnam. Kennedy said he did not want to negotiate with an enemy who still thought they could win. We rounded up the peasant farmers and put them behind barbed wire. We called it the Strategic Hamlet Program and its purpose was to protect the rural population, save and except the mishaps, from the bombs we were dropping, and communist insurgents. Sir Robert Thompson, of the British Advisory Mission to South Vietnam, coined the name and he assured the President that it would improve conditions for the local population. He never suggested we bomb the remaining villages but Texas warehouses were full to the brink from the Bolshevik threat. And every day we made more to match the rhetoric, rivalled only by our appetite for them new fangled blenders.

It was 1966 and we had not yet brought democracy to Indochina. No one now disputes the region had run out of options, not an easy thing to see, in a place that is foreign. In short, we did the talking while the people disappeared into a burning landscape. The poor cannot linger too long over a gravesite if they are to keep alive their contempt. Professor Rowe, director of graduate studies in international relations at Yale, suggested that America buy up all Canadian and Australian wheat to destabilize the Chinese economy. The Chinese would pull their support from Vietnam in the wake of mass starvation and, he assured the President, the Japanese would be pleased.

With Sisyphus I stood at the top of the hill, he smiled as we watched his boulder roll to the bottom. Kings perish but my work goes on, he said, I am learning what I have already done. Before I was informed of my mission I stopped in to see the Canadian Prime Minster. Canada is not to blame for all this, I could tell by their poetry. Nothing is more pointless than this great big nation and that includes Norway. From their beavers they know to keep busy. Its raison d'être is the standard of living and the abyss is more booze than you could drink in a sitting. Nature trails through mountains of raw material, well marked. You can walk for days and not find a skeleton. I handed the prime minister a list of what we would need to supply the next bloodbath. He smiled when he realized he could step up production. The rest, I said, we'll get from Australia.

Lately there's been nothing but earthquakes, drought in the remote provinces. One morning I woke up and the mouse was at the foot of my bed. I was dreaming about the nineteenth century, I said, philosophers in beards and greatcoats … Germans … I think so … they're the worst, what did they say … they said people are living forever and not a moment longer ... what does that mean ... it means we die in increments ... of what ... time ... I don't understand ... divided ... we do die, then ... yes, but we never get there ... idiots ... they seemed to know ... knowing has nothing to do with it ... I see ... what else did they say ... you do realize this is a dream ... answer the question ... the French came ... oh ... they argued … typical … the Germans took the high road ... obviously ... then what ... I woke up ... are you sure ... no.

My freedom is of a kind that is not here yet. I am blind to the thing that approaches, and the first time I saw my double is when he picked up a crayon. He is this trembling, or that's how I drew him. It's all gone badly and I think he's befriended the enemy, ruined the war and the economy. He has no aches and no body parts, such things would curtail his agenda and nothing is more durable than an idea. He says it's a joy to be alive and, apparently, I'm also fine. Then he hands me the crayon. The arrangement is not a bad thing, if it is a thing, more likely it's nothing, but that too is a reason. Last I heard he was face down in the Gulf of Mexico on his way to Houston or Galveston. I did nothing to help that boy, but I could have.

One night, before he made his escape, I asked my double if he had received his instructions and, what do you think of the war ... war is ruined by the people it leaves behind ... oh ... it's best not to say too much ... I see ... or just pretend it never happened ... that would be difficult ... not really ... oh ... it's standard protocol ... I see ... change the story and don't talk about the numbers ... fascinating ... present all sides ... that's very democratic ... call in the experts to disagree ... I see ... and keep your mind on your mission ... what is my mission ... your mission ended the day you were captured ... what is your mission ... to learn all there is to know and report back to the President ... I thought that was my mission ... I told you, your mission is over ... not according to the bird ... the bird doesn't exist ... neither do you ... your point ... I don't know.

The Hudson Institute concluded after much research that the Asian poor do not love life as we do. Theirs is to suffer and die. For us it is a terrible burden but death does put an end to their groping. Knock, knock, you're living in the wrong place and where you're going – that's ours too. I've already said everything twice, but between the same and the same there is a lot of discrepancy. I am not disheartened by how murky these words are, but by how little they distort. I'm trying, and trying helps me to steer clear of the ending. There is no difference between what I say and don't say but that which is missing is pleasing. I love all manner of slits, slots and slippage, and my philistine attention to alliteration.

In New York tragedy is a woman who never leaves her apartment. In Calabria it's a winter without mushrooms and chestnuts, or an earthquake. As a child I was instructed by nuns, which was good because they didn't let the monks touch me. Later I went to Harvard but the teachers couldn't get my brain to harden. Apparently I didn't know what the words meant, and no one believed me when I said they were arbitrary. I argued in favour of their chaste infinity, their spotless lack. Still do in fact, at my age it's important to preserve elasticity. Speaking of elasticity, a massacre at sea soon looks like a place where nobody died. On land it takes a little longer for things to settle, but if there's time to skedaddle do take your sister.

In 1980 the Mennonites wanted to ship grain to Vietnam. The President explained that hunger is someone else's predicament. We can stop them from organizing but we cannot help those who resist our aggression. In Cambodia the old are still dreaming of a little pork with their rice and the young are not living as long as they used to. The seasons too have yet to find this place again since it all changed, in an instant. So much depends on the weather. The napalm that fell in sixty-eight ruined the sixty-nine harvest, and for fifty years hence. Birds were the first to go with their music, followed by the fruit on every tree, but not so the people. They rounded up the scrap metal from the towns that we levelled and built the factories to supply Gap and Nike.

There is nowhere from which I cannot strike. This room or the thirteenth century, a castle in Hapsburg, such is the reach of my truancy. War and art will immortalize those who would have otherwise drowned in a bowl of soup. When I got here I was centuries late, God had already absconded. All that remained was my nonexistence and this face from which to carve my own likeness. This morning I set out to find the next page, then I reported back to the author. I am but a pawn who informs the king, but it's a rare king who listens. The next page too is all surface, I cautioned, but the scribbler couldn't hear me. No matter, his days are numbered.

In South Dakota they chiselled their kings into a mountain. In ancient Rome they were struck from white marble, skulls formally spaced like eggs in a carton. Everywhere there are severed heads, but a carving doesn't worry about an appendix bursting. In Guantanamo and in the dungeons below the coliseum prisoners improvised. I once heard a man admit he'd trained a rabbit to assassinate the President. That was a bad year for rabbits. There are places in this world where everybody confesses. Jesus, for example, told those charged with his torture of trains in Poland as far as the eye could see. But trains had not yet been invented so they killed him. A believer might disagree with the details but I won't change my story.

The Texas messengers are behind me, I didn't hear them come in. Have you arranged a meeting with the bird and the mouse … I don't think it's going to happen … why not … I can't control their coming and going ... oh ... nor yours for that matter ... what did they say ... they refuse to be in the same room at the same time ... why ... the mouse can't listen to the bird's speeches ... and the bird ... he says the mouse is corrupt ... what are the speeches about ... re-education ... have you heard them ... yes ... where was he ... in this room ... where specifically ... on the table ... who was here ... just me ... anyone else ... I don't think so ... are you sure ... no ... what have you told the mouse ... nothing ... why not ... I don't think he cares.

Persia no longer exists so I would like to live there. I want to go to where the future is over. There is no difference between what is and what isn't, but I prefer the latter. When slaves are forbidden to speak, they sing. In Louisiana their songs were a pause in a really dark night to steady a rotting eternity. I guess that's why they called it the blues. Masters build cities, hotels on the beach, schools, churches and prisons. They make sure everyone has something to sing about. Slaves know that Louisiana will perish someday, after I die I will live there. Songs follow the living but when they get here I'll explain everything. This is the future, I'll say, modelled after a New England town. Heaven had to start somewhere and the good book is clear, time without end of tepid duration, but now that you've come the next thing I'll invent is a gun.

Before the slap of freedom there is the smell of diesel. An interim government will deliver the beginning in the local dialect, so the people can decide the future. Words, through repetition, acquire their solidity, that's why they're impenetrable. This is chatter as chatter, from the inside of its own impossibility. Hakim tells me the BBC is over-reporting on Iraqi football, doing their part to make foreigners invisible. The empire kills everything twice but only one is final. Then they leave the way they came, dispensing chocolate to the children. No child frowns forever and confectionery trumps calamity. So say the psychologists. Life is a dream after furniture, cars and houses. From this room I see the moon, but it's not the one I wanted.

Last night I was visited by that unfortunate man I first met on page thirty-nine. But I doubt he'll still be there after editing and final formatting. I was in France at the time, on the beach, and he told me to drown in the ocean. Apparently he took a wrong turn and so we got to talking. Tell me, he said, do you have family ... I have a brother who's crazy and one who's a banker ... let's not split hairs. The man explained that he'd taken to giving speeches at midnight, all threats and no commas, ignoring all who pass by. He's looking for his first thought, and hoping to learn the secrets of the secret police. If he stops he will die. I am responsible for what I've become, he explained, but on this you can rely, nothing happens at Starbucks and the rest I'll concede to economic historians.

The bird is back. I didn't hear you come in ... stay alert, there's a war out there ... that's true ... keep your mind on your work and one eye on the Dutch ... why the Dutch ... why not ... am I Dutch ... this isn't about you ... yes it is. In 2002 the United States Congress passed the *American Service Members Protection Act* so we could storm The Hague if necessary. Bring our boys home before they can be prosecuted for war crimes. Then we invaded Iraq and Afghanistan. The Dutch are afraid, are we friends or foes, and who's next in line for a makeover. The bird says there's no difference between the two, but don't tell the Dutch ... why not ... they think we agree with them.

34

The cavalry threads a barren highway. Bullets whistle through sand, smoke, and like thunder split the hulls of Halliburton's empty trucks. If you get lost, check under the seat. An endless caravan behind mirrored sunglasses in pursuit of regular billing for cargo that is signed, sealed and never delivered. Texas is the penetration of all things missing. The emissary of what we're waiting for, amid hunger, its black tongue begging at road's edge. Who knew hate could be so tender. By all other accounts this is paradise, a modern legend for middlemen and contractors who still dream of Victoria's China seas. Land ho, open contracts and no taxes.

The mouse is back, full of insinuations. Tell it like it is or it won't lie still, he said ... there is nothing to tell, I count the stones beneath my feet and console a shadow that will soon hang on the wall opposite ... you are building a house between our ears ... I think it is you who have pitched a tent, mouse ... I am not here ... I thought that was the bird ... then I'm not who you think I am ... I see ... during breakfast, days, and habits you scanned the odds with as many eyes as in a peacock tail ... I was doing my job ... no one cares and you were let fall through an open window ... I'm dying, mouse ... your point ... I don't know ... take a lesson from the French, nobody does absence like they do ... is death French ... I think so.

I know from my subscription to *The New York Times* that the days are consecutive in Manhattan. When they announce my death everyone will know to start loving me, but I will no longer be the one they're looking for. Everyone gives up eventually is what Franco knew when in Spain he bombed the cemeteries. He was just making sure the dead were dead for good. Malaga in ruins was a fitting place for a poet but what might have been is not a lasting thing, it's just the wind. A poet has to invent the alphabet to pin down the particular, to fill the world with corpses, to kiss their bloodstained caskets.

I'm adapting to my desert home. I exist and if left unattended I will learn to do it daily. This prison cell is just a pause, a place to streamline my identity.

In 1986 Reagan sent me to Angola with Jack Abramoff and representatives from the Heritage Foundation. Later we were joined by the leaders of the Contras and Mujahedeen from Nicaragua and Afghanistan respectively. We came together to help Jonas Savimbi fight a war which had excellent prospects for De Beers. During the conflict the company spent eight hundred million dollars on illegal gem stones. A diamond is passed down through the ages because everything else is fleeting. Before Wall Street, diamonds were the best way to finance a campaign. A derivative is an accord between two parties that is contingent on a future outcome. It has no value and neither does a diamond. What's important, Reagan told Savimbi, is the agreement plain and simple. Then Savimbi went back to Angola and killed five hundred thousand people.

We are not lost. We live in the stead of those who would be here. We search the faces for the faces we once knew. They had much to do before the bullets intervened. Yesterday I heard the rusty cries of an alley cat. All knowing ceased, there is no word for half a death. Behind the wall a soldier swims her laps to preserve mind and body, sometimes this is Italy. She will have much to tell at water's end. She lives inside the direction of the world. She has it from her father and the Army will pay for junior college. There will be shame. Hers is the life that nations make, no gravesite elegy for the death she brings. But all of this we knew, sleeping children next to dead cats, slowly.

When I arrived in Kosovo it was raining. Before I left the President explained what is meant by *illegal but legitimate*. It is the pre-emptive privilege of a people who need not explain the death that follows their great mission. The President will come clean after he chooses his biographer. His biographer will say he lived in the service of the people that he killed. I am explaining everything to Hakim. He does not understand the ridiculous things I tell him. It was obvious from the dates on my laundry tickets, all of this would end, distilled to a few buried coins and a few random bones. Poets without knowing will have rewarded the disaster. It is not easy to understand the state, its crimes we will forgive because we must forget. Something in our speech is flawed, in all things – nothing.

As I've said elsewhere, after one o'clock comes two and so on, but I do wish the mouse would stop talking. The syllables are clear, his sentences impenetrable. In Germany before the war many women were well-endowed in spite of their hunger … why are you telling me this, mouse … after the war you had to close one eye to see them and there was a change in the government ... oh ... people lying beneath stretched skies and fallen bricks … I see … better for dreaming full breasts and hips on the veranda of the Hotel Adlon … what … in eyes up to my neck like stars not crushing me at all … slow down mouse … Berlin dumb and shining in the mud, asleep with panic … no more mouse … landscapes drowning inside troubled bodies ... stop ... I married a Christian bigger than a Portuguese church … you're going too far … if only that were possible.

Oh the places I'll go. After lunch and before dinner, in the middle of the nineteenth century precisely, I found myself on a mountain or in a tree speaking an obscure African tongue. It seems I had stumbled on some remote tribe. Their young etched and sleeping under stones. This is the death kings and fathers dream about, so they can always love you. How familiar it all seemed, and familial. That's my eldest, said the man they called the emperor, a warrior and an inspiration to his younger brother who's buried next to him. The king wore a greatcoat with epaulets. In Napoleon's France he'd be a great general but here he was just grotesque. He asked, and then forgot my name. I had decided on Bixby or Bray, he called me Mordecai. I left under cover of night lest he mistake me for the opposing king's daughter.

After a brief stopover in Portugal I made my way back to my room. Lisbon, I think I could tell from the postcard, in the shoebox underneath my bed. The Texas messengers were waiting for me, they came without sound, without warning having mastered the discipline of not being. I informed them that African kings were comforting themselves with whisky while children mutated. I suspect, I continued, our work there and elsewhere is the undertaking of an aberrant ego that fears life more than death. I have begun to talk to the water that seeps through the cracks in these walls and the time has come for me to go home with my song. The messengers handed me a rope and a note, told me to stop reporting on the weather.

In the time of time to come a people will roll up the sky to renew a legend but we are not it. It harkens back to a simpler time when we all agreed on the enemy. Our children's children will rummage through their dead, we must not disappoint them. Their world too will come undone. They are nostalgic for the old stories, the day we stormed Berlin and closed the furnaces. We must tell them despair is not an identity crisis in Manhattan, they will find themselves again in Santa Fe. Despair is a disease of the flesh and names that are holy cannot be trusted in this darkness. They have been spoken of in many ways and are not impossible to know, they are simply not. I will stay awhile amongst these artefacts that get dug up later.

In Texas what is loved by one is loved by many and then it changes. The President is insisting that I report everything that I see here, but what I see is not here or at least the here of what I see is not anywhere. He says he's no longer interested in my excuses and neither am I. My mind now sits in the palm of my hand and every day the empire sends a fiddler to thwart the rising complexity of my idiom. Who can blame them. Texas is more than what it does not think. It is the authority on scarcity elsewhere. Ditties, jingles and war cries from the cradle to the Super Bowl. Texas kneels to the cult of initiative that will adhere to invention and yield to expansion. Lack and an encore. If there's enough time I will repeat everything.

After a battle Texas sits down for a cold refreshing Coca-Cola, the British prefer tea. The home front keeps the books and the fire burning. How many must die to protect Connecticut. Here is how it works, on first blush with life's grim wish, confess, then enlist. War is good for everybody except the dead and the maimed. And it frees up real estate. In Vietnam a platoon could be isolated for days and weeks. The carnage was severe, but the boys just kept on jonesing. The army lied, but they didn't have to. If not there, then on the streets of Baltimore. The enemy is everywhere. So said the chaplain at Fort Worth on the day of their departure. He followed it with a Godspeed, or may the Lord protect you son. As to arrivals, he referenced the past tense.

Why do I have to die, bird ... we have need of your absence ... I can leave ... it's not the same. What I am telling you now has not been invented. I have yet to receive a message from Transylvania. My hallucinations fit inside a spoon which is over there. My wife wants a divorce. My son has moved to San Francisco, or Iowa. All I have left is this refusal with which to sway the court. I'm worried. I have begun to read a Chinese poet in Chinese. I do this on faith because I do not speak the language. He told me of a hummingbird that changed the world from deep inside the winter of a birch forest. I showed him the rope that Texas sent. I am in love with this world, he said, but I'm dumb as a stone.

35

Killing thousands of non-combatants is a public relations fiasco, unlike the destruction of dams, locks and bridges. Studies indicate the elimination of such targets does not drown people. The result is shallow flooding, and eventually mass starvation unless food is provided, which, as suggested by John Theodore McNaughton, Assistant Secretary of Defence during the Vietnam War, could be done at the negotiating table. Tragically Theodore died at the young age of forty-five in a plane crash two weeks before he was to become Secretary of the Navy. Many of his ideas have since been implemented but the man himself recedes in our memory. Like ashes, like those able engineers of Europe who coordinated an unprecedented network of trains not so long ago.

In Baghdad, children have given their throats to the wind and are drifting west like snakes through a wire. The future will come to this dead age, and winter will come to the valley. Those who perished will appear once more to identify the armoured columns that delivered the President's message. A scientist will wonder and raise a stone, torn from a farmer's field or from below a eucalyptus tree. He is trained to read the message in a bottle but he can't play the piano. A graveyard is not a place to rest, and should it appear empty and vast, that's just the music playing. To the trained eye, our friend the scientist's, for example, it is always full. Unearthed, a child's sandal, a sewing needle will bind these people to their cries. They will be marked with the blood of each other. This is the mercy Texas could not find.

No one knows what a beginning looks like. A few fishermen fleeing the tyranny of an empire mend their nets to prepare for new bounty on a distant shore. A ship's captain whispers rumours of plenty in a king's ear. A tower will focus the future and a gun will preserve its meaning. Fish and a country, rust in the water, the fallen armour of simple men who were not safe. This place was found, or chosen, then we took to the business of selling the ruins. For their sake I hope we don't find gold or uranium. The people's dreams cover the centuries like skin, barely a pause before their eyes empty in a moment just like this one. In a few hundred years there will be smokestacks everywhere and we'll be talking trash under the stars and a Budweiser canopy.

Hakim says the town in which I was captured is still there, people are protesting in the street. I told him about Berkeley in the sixties. It's the same, he said, except for the air raids and the improvised explosives, and we've had to shut down the cafés. Time will wrest the shrapnel from the palm trees and the birds will return en masse to a defeated war. The poor, for a time, will choose a star to sleep under, until Halliburton can rebuild the houses they were born in. It will be some time before they'll have to change a light bulb. There are no more roses outside the Green Zone, no flowers in the marketplace. But it doesn't matter, a flower's meaning only deepens while we're waiting. A time to plant, a time to kill. Turn, turn.

Texas I appreciate the opportunity to conclude. The smell of meat reminds me of where we've been. Lately words have been slowing me down. They move in clusters to explain that which is already lost in the finding. I wish I could stop writing the same sentence, show you two deaths at the same time. But I do not suffer words like Vallejo, in fact, they don't hurt at all. It's just this sentence that's blood-red, and so on. I move from the razor in the mirror to the corn flakes on the kitchen table, but you know this, Texas. The alternative is the alternative because we didn't choose it. The enemy can never be strange enough, in the fifties he looked just like us. There is no lie unless we can agree, though from time to time we turn the guns on each other, but we never compromise our politics.

Bury me in Calabria, Texas, in my mountain village anyone who's been to New York is a big shot. All should be said and in the ground a few days before I die so I have time to adjust. The library should be moved to a lower floor as mobility is likely to become an issue. The end of the world has been with us for several decades now, so I won't need any more books, but music may still be of interest. Of canvas, all seeing ended at the turn of the last century and proper lighting would be a challenge. I'm hoping to meet myself again in the future. In an invention perhaps, an idea without a blueprint, I'm tired of the replication. Art is the smoke, the vestige, not the thing, an explanation that explains nothing. But where or what could nothing be? All through history it's been a mystery, and sometimes it rhymes.

From my window I see a clock tower, Hakim has assured me it keeps perfect time. Yesterday, in the evening, I heard several explosions. I hid under the table. In the morning I looked out the window. The perimeter of the courtyard had been breached and riddled with shrapnel. Through the wall I could see the root structure of one of three massive palm trees, fully exposed, the trunk strangely suspended. Legs, I thought. On the ground an earring, a basket half filled with bloodied fruit that never made it to the evening meal. As mornings go, this one was not exceptional. I opened my eyes, looked around and left the situation. Hakim appeared late morning in traditional Muslim garb. I wore plumes and armour.

What am I to do with my shame, perhaps I'll put it off until summer when it can be served cold. The music and its maker dead on a carousel. Had I known what was in store I would never have endorsed life and happiness, an endless caravan on a scorched highway moving toward wind and rock. A city seems so much smaller when there's no place to hide. It empties but for the very old peeking from behind torn curtains. On the window sill are a few ripening tomatoes and a photograph. In an air raid clothes then flesh fall from the bone like melting wax, skipping all the steps in between. The clothes would have seemed ridiculous in the coming decade, and in two they'd be vintage. Funny how we didn't see it coming.

It's not the not knowing that bothers me, I just didn't want it to end. I wanted this story to be told by a king in the last stages of syphilis, and after consulting with a pig's ass. I wanted to tear the skin from the words, watch him scream when finally he understood his own plan. I want to read and remember that I was never here. I believe in freedom, before I went to work for the government I rolled my own cigarettes and spit on the factory floor. Now I am examining it all from inside a dream, from a shithouse at the lake where the trees are still standing tall as childhood. I'm trying to see what comes later. All will be astonished by my narrow escape, and the land will be deeded back to those we have massacred.

What shall we do with all those who live on the wrong side or our guns? Mountains of people scattered to tents and an open road Kerouac neglected to describe. Not a choice exactly, but a journey nonetheless. At night the expanse disappears and the moon rarely gives up its corpses. The sun too is calamitous. These are not American deaths I'm describing. Slow-moving footmen in Sunday attire standing next to hydraulic coffins. These are deaths we deliver from behind the Wormwood Star and later estimate they did not take place. They are not the end of anything. It is late and soon I must begin work on the history of my stupidity. A where without a whom, and not anywhere before I had already left. A blind parakeet in flight, I'm learning what I will never know.

In the next room God has trimmed his beard and is giving the same old speech. Hakim and the guards listen intently. I created hell, I hear his voice through the wall, it's not my fault if you weren't listening. He is explaining that the oceans are one big cemetery and love is the few huddled against the rest. His is the thought that does not yet think the unthinkable. He doesn't belong here. I attend all his speeches and send copies to my lawyer who lends money to the poor without their knowing. He is not well-meaning. He lives in the modern world and collects on every penny. He has promised never to tell me anything. I will never tell you anything, he said, and that's what I call service.

I tell myself the same things year after year, and then I write them down. This room was first a room and then a word, or the other way around. Such things do not reside in my deciding. I have a list of things to do, things I wanted to know some day. Some words find the window and fly off to topple England. If not for the Brits we'd all be French. Thank God for foreigners or there'd be no state. None of this matters to a grasshopper, but I can't be sure because I've yet to hear one speak. War breaks the living and buries the dead without will, without seeing. Things change, but only a little, there is no alibi and no elsewhere. We always remain at the scene of the crime. You hurry to hurry but you must go away to be, at these crossings. Truth is not told, it is made. Peace everywhere.

36

We are the conquered, a footnote to someone else's legacy, a number that could not be more stark. Tickle us with a knife and we blush. We find sanctuary in the aftermath, tenderness in the master's assertion. We bury our kin and wait for instructions. Texas, it's not lying if you believe it. Nothing you say will surprise anyone, and heaven help us should your version fail to prevail. It's an old story, life is a gift but not for the poor, and only the technology gets better. All of this will unravel in some other era, in the future the present will be easier to bear. Help us to understand, Texas. Hell, we'll reimburse you for the missiles you dropped on our heads. We are in need of a provisional coalition authority, our children have grown bloody and we are not above suspicion. We have been to the brink of refusal.

Texas, the universe is but the backdrop to your rising, so is Nicaragua, Iraq or Vietnam. Briefly, all other nations. What monotony modern conquerors must bear. Genghis Khan and Attila the Hun received only praise for the people they slaughtered. A great empire should not be reduced to low-intensity conflict. There is no valour, no romance in proxy. But, Texas, imagine the sales. Not to suggest this is solely a lust for money, or power. It's also the carnage. If only I could peek into your skull, examine its aspects. As you well know, it's no different than cracking an egg. The ovum, it's been said, is perfection itself but that doesn't interest me. I like the way it forms a zero to shore up the crisis inside.

I've petitioned the moon, meditated on crystals, or was it spirals. My mind has been broadened but I tire easily, and such things do not inform our arrangements. Texas, the polls are against us so they must be wrong. I repeat, to who will listen, all you have told me, but everyone here is too cynical to understand our objective. Complaints are just not important when they're someone else's. Besides, we don't speak the language. They claim this war is but a pretext. Why not try Idaho next time, we need a place to invade. There, says Hakim, we might do some good and it's important to secure the potatoes. In the Midwest we'll be praised for whatever happens. A body, arguably, is a tuber that will never sprout. Welcome Idaho, to everything.

Texas, why is Bechtel selling rivers by the glass and why do we bury the scraps before we go in? When planning an incursion the beginning is all-important, the Germans knew this when they put the blitz in krieg. All that matters happens in an instant. That's why we came in through the wall, though the door was wide open, and to dazzle the locals. In come the soldiers and down goes papa, look away, said mama, they threw him down the stairs as though there were no stairs at all. Who knew limbs could be so brittle. It was a lovely sky, is all mom remembers. One brave mouse heard the screams, stopped long enough to understand the situation. Unfortunately it was before mice could speak so he never reported it.

In my room beginnings and ends are simultaneous, and some get shot down over England. Dear Lord, let this be a warning, I do not love you and I'm fine with the prison I'm in. It welcomes all comers and Hakim is not finicky about my affinities. He knows what we came for, it's crude. Forgive the simple entendre and should you grow tired of all these abstractions feel free to come down and tell me. We both know this needs more editing. Speaking of which, I've identified a few problems with your own book that we should discuss. I should have told you before it went viral. Evenings are best, I'm hardly conscious and we'll avoid the day's comings and goings. Not too late, I spend my nights travelling. Past wars, Norman or Roman with a stopover in Kalamazoo.

I am who I was – a diplomat – and sometimes I speak for the dead. I thought of becoming myself, listed the pros and cons, nothing balanced so I absconded. Later I realized the stupidity of trying. When I look in the mirror I see the same man. At all other times it's just space but I can still feel my anus. Hakim has put him on film, a comedy, apparently, but the protagonist is not believable and his story still needs an ending. I've discussed all this with my keeper, together, I said, we can take down something bigger. At Harvard, for example, we can pluck out a President or two, thirty-odd years before they take the oath, and given current technology we don't need to identify the target exactly. The pre-emptive approach is regrettable and even more effective, if we take out the maternity wards.

The end of the world won't amount to much and there'll be no one to show you the door. I've said it before, look for the miracle elsewhere. Inside an apricot, is what I suggested on page twenty-six, subject to the usual caveats. But hurry, before Monsanto takes out a patent. When I was told of my pending death I knew it had already taken place because I was a witness for the accused. I understood death's encounter with death because I have gathered all the books but none have spoken of where the future has been. I had to devise a plan for myself, for all the monks in Rome and a few in Jerusalem. Time is the oldest myth and nothing testifies like a corpse, though all of its thoughts are indecent. It wants the light only. Please tell us what you saw of machetes in the grass, women facedown in a swamp, of children waiting inside rock and armed with the same old songs.

My death will be much longer than time but I will forget what I was sure to remember forever, a kiss and a bicycle. A river bends and then disappears, when I returned from Harvard no one knew who I was so I took a job that has never existed. I supplied liquor to the meagre, built castles in a fishbowl and wrote lists from the inside of your head. Thank you for shopping. On Wall Street they are forecasting famine and betting on the spread. Opportunity follows disaster. In the evening I retired to a river view, washed the dirt from my hands and from my perfect life. I bought it for a song, from the poor before they moved to Jersey. All that was missing, which I have since added, was the scented candles and the antique bed.

The world was built with stones and a handful of edible roots, under a canopy of stars each smaller than my thumb.

We invented silk and armour, the unfortunate and how to hang them from the neck so goes the morning. Yesterday I wrote a letter to the World Court informing them that I have decided to testify, after I die. Hakim will see to its delivery. Praised be the rain and every grain of sand, both will wash away the stain, but against a flying gunship there's no escaping the terror. Our boys lit up a van with two children in the back seat. A cat screamed, saw that the world was not coming to an end and carried on. It's their own fault, a soldier was heard to comment, for bringing their kids to a battle. That's right, said another.

The bird is back. I'm tired of his chatter, his ideas aren't worth anything, especially here, where the headlines are so awful. I wish he'd go where he could be more useful. What separates us is his persistence, rare, I suspect, since he died in New York. The Texas messengers are still looking for a meet, but the bird won't talk to the mouse and the mouse couldn't care less. Next time I'll do this alone, forego my need to be seen. It's almost the end and there are so many things I've not done. Every day I kick something loose, wrestle it to the page. That's how I know this is just exploratory. The bird, the mouse and the Texas messengers are insisting on their legacy. Conclude, they say, finish dying or set us free. This is just the story, I explain, a dry run, a punt. I don't see the point in heeding their advice, and it would ruin the book. I should never have invented them.

I am hearing sounds, words from my pillow so I grew a beard and started walking on all fours. Should Hakim ask the reason I'll cite gravity, or a better brand of oxygen. Anything to throw him off the trail, for what could the reason be? There is a woman who walks a dog that chases a cat that eats a mouse in the house where they all live inside a picture. She is learning the memory of a woman walking a dead dog. I guess this is what is meant by time in motion. To travel so little on so many legs, count them, the legs I mean. Fourteen. When I have a mind once more I will seek confirmation, call the animals by name and count their limbs again. My room and I will have returned to normal. I will forget that woman and her animals, but I'll keep the cat to chase away the bird.

37

I HAVE EXPLAINED TO Hakim that in Texas the eagle is affixing stars to the flag. He has eaten the eye of his red master and now guards the soda shop from the inside of a Buick while wearing mirrored sunglasses. It once circled the abyss certain of its unknowing and the stars were for locating the next mountain peak. I am travelling on a raft made of timber on the crooked lanes of a fast-moving highway. My hair is wrong and so are my shoes. I am telling stories first told by a fortune-teller that I predicted wrongly. Our ancestors fought the savages and wrote letters back to England. Wish you were here dear, it's not familiar at all but at least it's ours. Already we have cleared out the natives and nearly as many hectares. I'll call you the instant Alexander dreams up the telephone.

Had I known, I would have gathered up the population and drowned them in a water glass as they stepped off the Mayflower. I came to this country a prospector with a string of donkeys and a shovel, the poetry of women and whisky at the ready, or so I imagined. I wielded a flute, a drum and a gun with more poise than John Wayne at the Alamo. I was commissioned to repeat the past, but I might be wrong. Outside I can still hear the bombs bursting and that's how we bring in the future. On arrival I was attended to by a sergeant from Wyoming, who introduced me to a dead soldier inside a well and the old man who killed him. Later I met Aban and later still Hakim. Hakim doesn't understand me and Aban lived at the whim of the army. He never said, and I never asked what he did with the money.

In the beginning everything was fine. We were told which words to utter and which to swallow, the toilet paper too was standard issue. I moved about quietly so as not to awaken the locals to their predicament. The vaguely analogous, the quasi is how I explained their future, and how I decide where I'm going. Contiguous, one must assume, to where we've been. It wasn't long before I was troubled by everything. How the fine dust of concrete mixes with the scented oils on a woman's skin. Plant extracts, said Hakim, from the Tigris or the Euphrates. I was further distracted by what happens to bowels, livers and spleens within the radius of a new Texas pit. Mr. President, this is not the bonanza I came for.

All of this existed before it was written to be better forgotten. Hakim's film will expose where I have been. More importantly, I'll be a movie star. When the war is over we'll sell the rights, sit back and watch the accolades roll in. In Hollywood there is no difference between praise and money, and the film was inexpensive to make because it took place in one room. Height, length and width collided, and then disappeared. Let me say from the outset, there were no magpies or I'd have heard them speaking. Overnight everything sorts itself out, in the morning I begin to pace again. Wait for Hakim, the bird or the mouse. I count on them for my best lines. It's a tentative narrative, trapped in its own circularity. I do what I can to ignore the protagonist. He has no script for the day after, and without that, there can be no disaster.

In my room there is a fly, there is always a fly, it comes, it goes and brings me nothing. We do not speak. This formality is sensible given the condition of pending death. Sometimes I imagine the war is over and I am reacquainted with the taste of apples in September, that buildings are buildings and not mountains of rubble. For Texas life always begins again, without knowing, without regret. CNN gives equal weight to every departure, all argument in rapid fire. It's more effective than a Chinese blackout, but only one is repressive. I am a hostage, held to account, the assurance of a promise that will not be made. Each morning the sun rises, witness to a death that will never arrive. Terror grows and then guffaws, but why must it be me and not the onion that cries.

I lied about Harvard but I have been to Hollywood. They are both in Texas. On the other side of these walls a people are collecting their rage, they are losing the war and forgetting to breathe. In Texas we are building machines to change the explanation, we are planning the church picnic. Paper lanterns hang in the trees powered by a gas generator. We must never succumb to the darkness. A child was born and later murdered, we had our reasons and besides, he forgave us. Bombing Muslims, Asians or anyone for that matter just makes his dying more meaningful. Still, one shouldn't bring an RPG to a picnic, sidearms are considered sufficient. Violence is order, and the other way around, beef is on the menu, Idaho spuds and Iowa corn. Later, God himself will take us to the river.

I am a responsible man. Responsibility is our gift to Texas, which is not ours to give. Good breeding is at the heart of murder. I came here to replace one myth with another, nothing lasts forever. Still, you can imagine my surprise when I was told it would cost me my hide. The bird knows this is wrong, or so I assume, but he is refusing to help me. He claims he's only here to gather intelligence. I give him plenty of information but not the kind that he's after. Perhaps that's the problem. I only invented him so that I could stick out my tongue. He's obsessed with the government, odd in a bird, but that's why he can't hear me screaming. The more noble the question the bigger the mix-up, is what I told Socrates. He was here this morning, said he regrets his decision. I thought it would be better, he explained, than no reason at all.

The Egyptians invented concrete to bury their kings. Water mixed with lime and sand, the long arm of a pharaoh's dream. All we do, we do for nothing, such is the other side of our failure and the destination unclear. We are slow to drown though we begin immediately. Not today, but soon I will break the stutter. The people we spare and the people we kill are the same. Everybody with money has left the city and cabbies don't even try to stay awake anymore. This is the beginning now. The dead will be required to attend public meetings, as one and many, and before they merge with roots and berries. A reunion absent the names, is how I like to think of it. First I'll be a mountain and then an ocean in my immortality.

All who visit this room, real, dead or imagined, acknowledge me as the architect of the new order. It is a daunting responsibility and so on arrival I began immediately to dismantle the region. Cities are easily rearranged but I'm having trouble rethinking the desert. After the revolution I will go again to live amongst rocks, someplace familiar, just me and the weather. British Columbia perhaps, before there were neighbours to care for or murder, before death and grammar. Not knowledge exactly, just trees and a river that was, and rabbits. In the beginning God favoured rabbits, and then he realized the king could broaden his tether. But the bunnies didn't mind because soon after there was a proliferation of lettuce. When I invent the new alphabet lettuce will be lettuce already.

One morning is the best I can do, for I awoke without adjectives. Suffice to say there was enough light to know I was being taken back to the room with the camera. Behind the lens I imagined Texas, for I knew they could see me, that we were together again. I was positioned by the artist Hakim. He handed me some text, life and death are the same word is what I read, and something about changing my mind. Clearly the work of a madman. I took the opportunity to ask Hakim when I will die. Soon, he said. My executioner stood askance, hooded and brandishing a beautiful sword. In the proper use of a tool one sees only the wound. In my room there is a new pattern, diagonal, eleven paces. I'm sure it's the one, when I am returned I will record the details. Why can't you see the world needs me, Hakim.

After the filming Hakim took me back to my room. Apparently my death was still being negotiated. I resumed my pacing immediately, tripped over bits of old stories. Try as I might I could not change the results. Always the same direction, inevitable like the tide when it gets hold of a corpse. Sometimes there is no escaping the truth, but it's not good for the phrasing. There is an apple waiting to refute a blossom inside a seed whose assertion is the tree. There are songs about loss that will not go away. I put my tongue on the floor because I wanted to put my tongue on the floor. Then I put my tongue on wood. I put my tongue on wood and on the floor. A madman invents the moment before it arrives and then waits for it to end. Everything takes too long.

Napalm is a jelly obtained from the salts of aluminium, palmate and naphthenic acids. When mixed with gasoline it takes on a consistency, a viscosity to good effect, stable and not too costly. For best results the bomb should fall rapidly from low altitudes, giving, by momentum, a greater length to the surface covered. The way to escape the asphyxiating effects of napalm is to flee into the open air where direct destruction by burning is assured. A battle will give up its dead, sometimes a name or at least the body parts. War is a rolling statistic, the President's moment to shine, and the lives that death gives birth to. Ours is to kiss the enemy, on both cheeks if you're French, and endure the centuries.

The President lives next to an apple tree by the mulberry bush. There is the sun peeking through the trees in a faraway land where children play but can't drink the water, scatter before they are cooked in their skin, thin, like that of a butterfly. The President's house is an enchanted place with velvet gardens on the banks of a river where all memory empties. From his bedroom window he can see the Appalachian foothills and in September he can see the ducks flying south for the winter. The mountains are magnificent from a distance but up close he feels his own insignificance. That's how it is with big things that are vertical. From these heights the river too is no more than a trickle, next to tunnels filled with the splash of a Texas night in fifty gallon drums.

The problem with democracy is the wrong people may get elected and our interests must not be encumbered. Should Wall Street fail, the people and all client states will empty their coffers. Order will be restored from behind the clouds, and a spattering of diplomats. We call that plan A, for abundance, there is no plan B. I used to sleep between a wink and a smile, but lately I turn in fully clothed. Sleep tight to the wall as per the advice, the annotations of a Russian poet transcribed while he was travelling through Asia. Soon after he was swallowed by an octopus, or before. The wall, he reasoned, made it more difficult for anyone to swing an axe at your head.

38

Hakim is very quiet this afternoon. I assume the date has been set for my execution, but he says it's not about me. What else is there, what else can there be. I am the gap in his line of vision, the same man in general. An I grasping an it, is how I'd put it if I still liked Levinas. I think it's the it that's the problem, and why I'm in this predicament. When the time comes I'll introduce him to the executioner. These crumbs will not reach infinity, this heaping in perpetuity is the wrong itinerary. It's unfortunate because I was just getting started. My day trips to the courtyard are also less frequent, meals are bland and the presentation haphazard. Hakim is no longer interested in learning English. As for my other visitors, the bird, the mouse and the Texas messengers, for example, I just made them up.

On the eve of all great massacres and before the first casualty, the President speaks to his blood-making boys by way of repetition. Which is good enough here. He says when there is something, there is always something else, anything can happen between now and then. If there is nothing it must be destroyed where it lives lest it drift. On the eve of all great massacres there is nausea, a bracing in the stomach to prepare for the victims' arrival, dead or starving on distant shores. This is nothing from the start. Let me explain, birth is an immense work of dispensation and murder in the name of a father, dead and rotting in all tongues where bodies wait to be massacred, tortured, infected, prostituted, starved, shot and piled outside my window.

The best way to dispose of a body is immediately. If it should disappear before having read Shakespeare so much the better. Such, we will say, was the distance between us. A catastrophe is not a catastrophe unless it undermines the economy. Calamities that never happened make the best stories. The future will round up the victims, and CNN will find a way to present them so as not to disturb the living. From his window the President is reminded we shoot ducks in autumn, but there's no season for people. Everywhere there are births aplenty in countries he's never visited. The President knows too much and too little. Eventually those who disappear return as numbers immortalized in the empire's literature, ledger or both. A canvas will distort the aggregate, though some would think otherwise. Dissent is healthy in a free society. It keeps us from knowing we're all drawing from the same inventory.

A tomb is built from the inside, or from wherever the light is receding. I am missing but I have mass and speak only to touch. The truth will not set you free, but to be clear, ask somebody else. Step lightly and poke them first with a stick. The French would agree with me, I can tell from their cynicism, but the Germans are encumbered by gravity. The rest is a game of cat and mouse with the alphabet, a forced march to the end of modernity. I've heard rumours the moon has been visited, the first note has been harnessed. It's only a matter of time before another onslaught of poetry. If only Condoleezza had taught me to play the piano. I'd forego the keys and use the hammers directly.

Every morning I clear my throat and prepare to give my report. I take my inspiration from what I imagine was said in my absence, or the light bulb, but I pretend it's a star. I wish I could say more, but all who pass through this room are reluctant to speak, or they never stop talking. I could do with the starting pitch, but I'd prefer a touch from a stranger. I hope she's a dancer. There's no there for death, not even – a there is not. Forgive the confusion, the word should have been stricken, it does nothing for our situation. This is a mishap correlated on a trash heap. Here absence becomes flesh and subject to fever. There's nothing we can do for you here, beat it kid, and check in with us later.

Before they cut off my head will I be able to wrap things up? To finish I mean. Is there time in that moment to finish? Should I stop finishing now, this leaking, this blood and piss? First mother, and then everything else goes missing is how Freud explained it. He was an expert, you see, that's why he did all the talking. As for myself things are more simple. I find what I say inside saying it, but it's not there when later I reference the sentence. A little time and some late night howling is all I have to kill a vacuum. It feels right and the sounds I'm making I've heard before in Abu Ghraib, or Guantanamo. But they wouldn't exist if I didn't write the last sentence. Without the words does Texas still know, premeditatedly I mean?

In New York the dog people streamed by my window with a menacing geometry. There was an office for the words. We were diplomats, you see. We always agreed on breakfast and sought those who also worked to agree. Be it an earthquake in Japan or a crop failure in Africa, there's a buck in everything. Leonard Cohen thought it was a crack. While in New York I don't remember if I remember talking about this room. On Tuesdays, I think, it was my turn to be wrong, see the good and the bad in some brutal government. It was comforting to know what the rooms were for. The words went back and forth, and money went into accounts discreetly. The talking was the thing, that's how it is with money.

I have not slept in fifty years. The questions in these answers chill me to the bone. The west wind always brings disaster. The locals gather to round up the scraps, for bits of news that we've discarded. They adapted long ago and are now partial to all things new, or newish from L.A. If it's worth selling, it's worth selling twice is what I told the President. In this country only the old can still afford their fury, from a distance and so long as they don't interrupt our dinner. They are complaining about the dirt on their shoes and all the people they must bury. Apparently we are accountable for what lies beneath every grain of sand, and before us it was the English. Long live the Queen and her special forces. A ceasefire is the perfect time for a cricket match. Late afternoon is best because we'll not redeem the night, and in the morning we must march.

As a child I understood I would be somebody else forever. Musing is how I take my leave, and it helps me breathe. In any case I did the work to hasten my departure, later my eyes closed, and opened. This is called learning. Texas, when dread next comes to call, let us introduce you. We have been known to rise to a catastrophe, genocide in the Sudan, an earthquake in Messina, an identity crisis in Hollywood. Baghdad burns, elsewhere lava cools. On the *Titanic* a ragtime band played a hymn as the ship was sinking, *Hold me up in mighty waters – Keep my eyes on things above.* They did not drown. They froze to death in waters next to the biggest ship since the beginning of the world.

Texas, we need you to bend to the sadness of a thin day. You come to every meeting with a briefcase full of countries, scatter wounds to the many that each must bear. You tell us who is sleeping with whom and who tops the charts. Thanks to you we are always up to date, but don't forget to pass on the savings. What have we to do with this place, we have so few dead and they have so many. Still the guns, Texas, and the enemy will drown you in a kiss. The death you bring is rising, and changes before it hits our mouths. When the time comes you always know what to say. Things are just easier when you rule the world.

Last night I dreamt an infant died. He fell from a rooftop. I picked him up and he disappeared in the palm of my hand, slowly and before my eyes. He's gone. I can turn now, stillborn, to where I am missing. My son, in New York I muttered something about constancy and service. I said that you would know Texas, in time, of time, in sequence with a telling known. But we do not know and you are not safe. The truth is worse than the telling. Yet these are not words to defeat you. Dread opens the sky. We are afraid, you and I have come this far. Let us count the bodies and commence to pray. I will not forget and I will never know, I will not forget and I will never know, I will not forget and I will never know…

Long ago houses fell in this valley, now woodlands bloom and a wolf sleeps in the thicket. Music is assembling space above the body's edge. It's for the birds. Texas needs the death penalty to kill its own. We have been watching you for centuries, and there have been such moments but we are in good health and no longer troubled by your arrival. We are cutting onions for the evening meal. The table is set and we will uncork the wine precisely one hour before your arrival. Do not be ashamed, Texas, we know what you have done and what you will do next. In the return of an infinite distance others will go on, nourished by this morsel that is our end. Sacrament given and received, killing is village living.

In the morning I asked the furniture to show me the night before. I retraced my steps, examined surface and mood, but it was not to be found. What we touch is not what remains. It had returned to its disappearance. Words are a scatter to look through but everything must first be missing. The violinist comes and speaks to me of my affliction. This room is not a situation, he says, it is the fingerprint before the touch. You will never leave and you will have never been here. I am arranging things, I cannot help myself. My death will not happen because it has already happened. I remember, but enough about Texas.

In San Francisco the streetcars chime, in New York too they have no idea that I have come undone. Perhaps I should renegotiate with my captors, adjust to this place since it's no longer foreign. Forego my organs and the very next metaphor, hitch a ride on a parable. I'll throw in my Manhattan condo, an incentive to extend the lease on my current quarters. Stall, until the work is finished, evolution that is, of the species. The world in ruins, an end to the search for perfect governance. I am clearly dumbfounded by all that has happened, but I'm fine with that. On the last day even a stick-figure will find its expression, develop an ear for the guttural sounds. On that day I will still thirst for what I can only know then. Imagine my surprise when I realize, I was happy to be here.

http://moredeathandtexas.com/

Composer: Grant Curle

Acknowledgements

Excerpts of this book first appeared in *Rampike Magazine*, and later in *Exile Literarary Quarterly* (*ELQ*), *Italian Canadiana*, University of Toronto. The author wishes to thank their editors.

I also acknowledge, with thanks, the extensive and exhaustive input from Chris Marks.

Francesco Lorrigio for his translation, to appear in an Italian anthology in 2013.

Lastly a note of thanks to Susan Walker for final edits, and those early, all important readers including; Tim Conley, Maurice Elliot and Ruwa Sabbagh.

About the Author

Claudio Gaudio was born in Calabria, and lives in Toronto.

Quattro Fiction

A Certain Grace by Binnie Brennan
Life Without by Ken Klonsky
Romancing the Buzzard by Leah Murray
The Lebanese Dishwasher by Sonia Saikaley
Against God by Patrick Senécal
The Ballad of Martin B. by Michael Mirolla
Mahler's Lament by Deborah Kirshner
Surrender by Peter Learn
Constance, Across by Richard Cumyn
In the Mind's Eye by Barbara Ponomareff
The Panic Button by Koom Kankesan
Shrinking Violets by Heidi Greco
Grace by Vanessa Smith
Break Me by Tom Reynolds
Retina Green by Reinhard Filter
Gaze by Keith Cadieux
Tobacco Wars by Paul Seesequasis
The Sea by Amela Marin
Real Gone by Jim Christy
A Gardener on the Moon by Carole Giangrande
Good Evening, Central Laundromat by Jason Heroux
Of All the Ways To Die by Brenda Niskala
The Cousin by John Calabro
Harbour View by Binnie Brennan
The Extraordinary Event of Pia H. by Nicola Vulpe
A Pleasant Vertigo by Egidio Coccimiglio
Wit in Love by Sky Gilbert
The Adventures of Micah Mushmelon by Michael Wex
Room Tone by Zoë Garnett